He launched on ~~~~~~~ ~~~ but Antonluca stopped listening.

Because all he could think about was timing.

Two and a half years ago.

Already pregnant.

What were the chances...?

But he knew that chance had nothing to do with this.

He didn't need to hear another word from this weasel of a man. He needed to hear it from Hannah directly. He needed to *know*.

Because down deep in his bones, as if his DNA recognized what it was being told without a single shred of proof, he was already sure.

Hannah had a child.

And if Hannah had a child after the night she had given her innocence to him in New York, well.

He was absolutely certain, sight unseen, that it was his.

USA TODAY bestselling, RITA® Award–nominated and critically acclaimed author **Caitlin Crews** has written more than one hundred and thirty books and counting. She has a master's and PhD in English literature, thinks everyone should read more category romance and is always available to discuss her beloved alpha heroes—just ask. She lives in the Pacific Northwest with her comic book–artist husband, is always planning her next trip and will never, ever read all the books in her to-be-read pile. Thank goodness.

Books by Caitlin Crews

Harlequin Presents

Her Venetian Secret
Forbidden Royal Vows
Greek's Christmas Heir
Her Accidental Spanish Heir
Forbidden Greek Mistress

The Teras Wedding Challenge

A Tycoon Too Wild to Wed

The Diamond Club

Pregnant Princess Bride

Notorious Mediterranean Marriages

Greek's Enemy Bride
Carrying a Sicilian Secret

Work Wives to Billionaires' Wives

Kidnapped for His Revenge

Visit the Author Profile page at Harlequin.com for more titles.

AN HEIR FOR CHRISTMAS

CAITLIN CREWS

PRESENTS

If you purchased this book without a cover you should be aware that this book is stolen property. It was reported as "unsold and destroyed" to the publisher, and neither the author nor the publisher has received any payment for this "stripped book."

ISBN-13: 978-1-335-21326-6

An Heir for Christmas

Copyright © 2025 by Caitlin Crews

All rights reserved. No part of this book may be used or reproduced in any manner whatsoever without written permission.

Without limiting the author's and publisher's exclusive rights, any unauthorized use of this publication to train generative artificial intelligence (AI) technologies is expressly prohibited.

This is a work of fiction. Names, characters, places and incidents are either the product of the author's imagination or are used fictitiously. Any resemblance to actual persons, living or dead, businesses, companies, events or locales is entirely coincidental.

For questions and comments about the quality of this book, please contact us at CustomerService@Harlequin.com.

TM and ® are trademarks of Harlequin Enterprises ULC.

 Harlequin Enterprises ULC
22 Adelaide St. West, 41st Floor
Toronto, Ontario M5H 4E3, Canada
www.Harlequin.com

Printed in Lithuania

AN HEIR FOR CHRISTMAS

CHAPTER ONE

HANNAH HANSEN MADE her way into work one morning that December fairly *bursting* with the holiday spirit.

Part of it was the gorgeous Italian scenery that beckoned from every direction. The hills were browner this time of year, the skies less gold and blue, but Hannah thought that only made the magic of Tuscany more apparent. That magic was in the mist that clung to the hills and the church steeple. It was there in the quiet stone streets of the hilltop village she drove through today, the one she was coming to consider her home. This was a magic that was right here, all year long, stamped down into the earth like its long history even when the bustle of tourists was gone.

There was something about Italy in the cold that made her heart ache in all the best ways.

Especially during the Christmas season.

It had been a difficult decision to leave the United States behind three years ago. It wasn't something Hannah had ever imagined she would do, but then again, there were a lot of things about the last few years that she never could have imagined in advance.

This morning she had left the best of those things—her son, the sweet and good-natured Dominic—playing merrily with his toys in the care of the marvelous Cinzia. Cinzia, who had started as the landlady, had become the very best neighbor imaginable. And she was now, for all intents and purposes, the family Hannah had always wished she had.

Instead of the family she did have, all of them still clustered together in a scrum of judgment and shame in a tiny town outside of Omaha, Nebraska.

The prospect of Hannah having a baby out of wedlock had scandalized them all. *How can we hold up our heads at the market?* her sister had asked once.

In all seriousness.

This and many other similar interactions were why Hannah had decided, at six months pregnant while she still had some savings left, that she deserved better than being treated like the blackest of black sheep in the state of Nebraska. With a set of scarlet letters to boot.

And she had always dreamed of going to Italy one day, because didn't everyone? So she decided that *one day* had come. She'd bought herself a one-way ticket to Florence, the city that had inhabited her dreams for as long as she could remember. She'd wandered about *piazzas*, ate too much gelato, and spent too many nights in lustily robust *trattorias* before making her way to a tiny little village out in Tuscany's undulating hills that felt familiar the moment she saw it. As if she'd always been meant to find her way here.

Aside from the *fate* aspect of it all, she was pretty sure she'd read about this village once, back when she'd still been living in New York City.

New York City.

She shivered a little as memories of that frenetic, exuberant city and her time there washed over her once again. The way it always seemed to do no matter how many times she assured herself that she was done looking back.

Hannah blew out a sigh as she navigated her way through the narrow streets of the ancient village that clung to the side of the hill, stones steeped in thousands of years of history. She followed the winding road down toward the fields again, and tried to breathe deep a few more times as she headed up another rolling hill on the far side.

It was hard to imagine on crisp and beautiful December mornings in Tuscany, far away from any sort of city, that she'd ever lived in the thrilling, overwhelming, concrete sprawl of Manhattan. Like she was remembering a television show, not her own life. Because those short, busy, overwhelming years seemed like not just a different life entirely, but something she might have dreamed up one night. One of those dreams that didn't go away in the morning, but lingered on forever.

"And then ended poorly," she muttered to herself as she crested the hill, lest she forget the crucial part of her Manhattan years.

Though Dominic made up for pretty much anything and everything that might have happened before his birth.

But she stopped thinking about the past then, because the view before her opened up again.

She sighed again, but happily this time, the way she always did at this point in her drive to work from her darling cottage on the other side of the village. Because there, lolling across the spine of the next rolling Tuscan hill, was the estate.

Not quite a castle in any classic sense, it was a collection of manor houses strung along the hillside like a necklace fit with jewels that some indolent Italian noble had tossed aside on his way to some or other Renaissance. Once the home of a succession of minor nobles, the estate had fallen into disrepair by the early twentieth century. It had been bought and toyed with by one optimistic and/or wealthy individual after the next since then, because the vineyards still produced rich red wines and the cypress trees still marked the age-old roadways. It was a place that seemed half sky, half ancient earth, strung round with olive groves, lavender, and vines of determined wisteria.

But a place like the estate required vision to fully resurrect, and so it had stood dormant for some time.

In the village, they called the attempt to launch a pile of stones and abandoned houses into something luxurious *una follia*, a folly.

Nonetheless, some ten years ago, the wife of the extremely wealthy Italian businessman who had recently claimed the place had taken it as part of her divorce settlement. She had then renovated the whole of the estate, transforming it into a hotel that exuded style from every newly polished stone. La Paloma, as both she and the estate were known, was infamous for her deep delight in taking petty revenge on those she felt wronged her—meaning, all of her ex-husbands, and she'd racked up a fair few—as well as her architectural flair and eye for design.

Hannah had walked into the hotel a scant ten days after she'd arrived in Italy, the gluttonous week in Florence behind her, because she knew she needed to find a job. She had driven into this village, overcome with that sense of homecoming. She'd eaten in the tiny trattoria in town, and had watched the old men gather in the square. She had stayed in a *pensione* a bit of a walk from the center of the village, and it was while walking back to her room that she'd seen the estate on the hill.

It was so beautiful. That had been her first thought.

When she'd learned that it was a hotel, she'd been thrilled. Because she could work in a hotel. It had to be better than a restaurant. Because anything was better than the nightly chaos of a restaurant.

She had pled her case to the hotel manager when she'd presented herself at the front desk, though she glossed over the reasons she'd left her last position of managing a Michelin-starred restaurant in New York. She'd focused more on the fact that she'd worked in hospitality for her whole career. And more, that she had just moved to the area and would be delighted to work in any potential open position he had—because it was clear that La Paloma was destined to become the uncontested gem of the region, polished as it was to such a bright and glorious shine.

But the hotel manager had looked at her belly, sneered, and only then looked her in the face. *Perhaps* la signora *should be at home with her husband, awaiting this most blessed event. This would surely be a better use of your time.*

He did not say *and mine*. Though it was heavily implied.

La Paloma had descended upon them then, appearing in a cloud of scent and fury as she wafted her way into view. She was a formidable woman in every regard. She was the kind of skinny that was best suited by bespoke couture garments from ateliers in places like Milan and Paris, all of which hung perfectly on the sort of ruthlessly emaciated body that was more an advertisement of determination and self-control than any aesthetic. She had waved one bejeweled finger at the hotel manager.

Perhaps you should take your own advice, Raffaele.

And that easily, Hannah was hired.

La Paloma, champion of women though not one to go easy on anyone, had tossed Hannah directly into the deep end. She'd informed Hannah that she had two weeks to figure out the manager's job and to excel at it. If she managed this feat, the position was hers. Complete with maternity leave.

That is remarkably kind, Hannah had said in sheer wonder as the furious Raffaele took his leave.

I'm never kind, La Paloma had told her, her dark eyes gleaming. *But I like to think that I can spot a diamond in the rough, my dear girl. And I know how to make one gleam.*

As if the diamonds dripping off of her didn't tell the same story.

Hannah, obviously, had made certain to exceed the older woman's expectations.

When Dominic was born, she had taken a month of leave and then had returned to work. She stayed mainly in her office so that she could keep the baby with her as much as possible and tend to what matters she could from there, since the guests certainly did not need to see the hotel manager's private, domestic affairs.

When he was six months old, Cinzia had offered to watch Dominic whenever Hannah was working, and that was that.

She had somehow stumbled into this beautiful little life that fit her well, made her happy, and as far as she could discern, could not possibly be better in any regard. She loved what she did. She loved the hotel, was eternally indebted to La Paloma, and enjoyed the demands of her position and all the problem-solving it entailed.

Best of all, no one in the hotel was in the habit of flinging food in her direction, like the overwrought chef she'd had to contend with back in New York.

Tuscany might have been like a dream, but these days it was Hannah's dream come true.

She parked her little car in its usual place in the staff parking area, and stepped out into the chill of the morning.

It was lovely and quiet today, with a cold wind dancing high above and scrubbing the sky clean. The hills rolled away toward the horizon, a more muted green than their summer splendor, but that did not make them any less beautiful. While she'd grown up in Nebraska, she often dreamed of places like this. Magical places so far away from what she thought of as real life. Fairy tales made real, and beautiful, in sophisticated settings far, far away from her small town life.

Her family had always teased her for that, and not always good-naturedly. They'd loved nothing more than to tell her that the real world wouldn't be kind to a girl who lived and breathed fantasies the way she did.

So she'd proved them wrong, obviously.

She'd gone to college and found her way into the hospitality field. They had expected her to return home, and possibly move as far away as Omaha, a solid forty-five-minute drive away from her childhood home. They had all found it flashy and tasteless that she'd instead gone off to a terrible din of a place like New York City. And worse, had dressed like the sort of person who would be successful in New York City—*as if you really think you're going to make it*, her sister had said one Thanksgiving with a derisive laugh.

But of course she felt that way. They all felt that way. They found it *unimaginable* that Hannah started off right out of college working in hotels so luxurious that no one from her entire hometown could imagine that anyone would spend that much money on a single night's stay. Much less go to a restaurant that charged even more.

Hannah had learned to downplay her initial run of success because they all found even that garish and showy. Or maybe it was that they thought *she* was.

At a certain point, she thought now, she'd had to accept that the common denominator in the things her family didn't like about her…was her.

Something that had become very clear and impossible to ignore when she'd gone home after losing her job at the restaurant.

She stood where she was, there near the parking area that was part of an ancient forecourt. In every direction, she was surrounded by the hills of Tuscany, the trees that seemed almost like heather this time of year—dressed in russets and deep autumn colors—and the winter vineyards slumbering in the cold ground. It was a sunny day now, if cool, with the morning mist burning off even as she watched.

Hannah took a deep breath, as if blowing it out again could scrape her family directly out of her system. That little sniff her mother liked to make. Her sister's arch, judgmental asides. Her father's quiet disapproval.

The fact that not one of them had reached out after

she left at six months' pregnant. She'd been the one to let them know that she'd settled in Italy when, three weeks after she'd left, there still hadn't been so much as a text.

For all they knew, she'd been living rough somewhere.

Of course you've moved to Italy, *of all places*, her mother had said with a sniff. *Typical Hannah.*

It had baffled her then. It still did.

Though there was no mystery as to why she was thinking about them *now*, she acknowledged. It was December. Christmas was coming. And despite her very real and very hard feelings about the way they'd treated her—and had always treated her—try though she might, Hannah couldn't bring herself to love them any less.

Especially at this time of year.

"Love doesn't mean full access," she murmured to herself. The way she often did because it was supposed to be soothing. "I can love them from afar."

She called home every Sunday and made herself suffer through the usual stilted conversation, in which her parents acted as if she'd had their grandchild simply to spite them. She'd stopped asking them to come visit, because they wouldn't. But Dominic deserved to know his family, she reasoned, and to make his own decisions about whether or not he wanted them in his life. She couldn't make that decision for him.

Maybe, she liked to tell herself, she would stop calling one day. But deep down, she knew that if she did, she would never hear from them again. Something about that continued to hurt too much.

"One day," Hannah promised herself under her breath, "it won't hurt at all."

One day.

But today, there were far more exciting things to think about than tired, old family dynamics.

She smoothed down the front of her dress as she walked toward the entrance to the hotel, swinging around to the front of the main building because she always liked to get a sense of the place as if it was new. As if she was a guest arriving for the first time.

The main building looked like an ancient fort built around a bell tower, though the old stone gleamed these days. The entrance itself was wide and welcoming, with evergreen displays wrapped in lights as a nod toward the season. Even looking at it made her feel peaceful.

This was how Hannah wanted the whole hotel to feel.

This was particularly how she wanted this Christmas season to feel.

And so it will, she assured herself as she walked. She adjusted her flowy, soft wool wrap on her shoulders and gripped the leather folder in her hand tightly.

La Paloma was a woman of many projects and a deep well of boredom. Or so she had told Hannah one night as they sat together in the finest suite in the hotel, which was, of course, the only place she would stay when she visited. She served only vodka gimlets and insisted that anyone who she invited to join her drink up.

And Hannah had never met anyone who argued with La Paloma.

I've sold the hotel, her benefactress had told her.

It had been two weeks ago now, out of the blue. But that was La Paloma.

But don't fret, my dear girl, I have made your continuing employment condition of the sale. To tell you the truth, I think you will be delighted.

Hannah had spent a lot of time working with the older woman over the past couple of years. She was not *quite* as overawed by La Paloma as she had been at the start. But that didn't mean she didn't maintain a healthy level of respect. This was the only reason that she didn't respond immediately to express how extremely *not delighted* she was by this development.

This place is special to me for many reasons, La Paloma had continued, waving her gimlet in the air the way she liked to do, for drama and emphasis. Not that she ever spilt so much as a drop. *Not least of which is that it was once a prize possession of my ex-husband, upon whom we wish every last thing that he richly deserves. But it is also unique in that it gave me something of a blank canvas, and I find that what I have done here has pleased me excessively. In every possible way.*

She had sighed then, as if congratulating herself. *I knew that I could not sell it to the typical portfolio-hoarding financier, or any other such person. It could only be a friend.*

Hannah had made herself smile. *With apologies,*

madam, but I was under the impression that you did not suffer friends.

Paloma laughed. *So needy. So grasping. But no, darling, I'm a great fan of friendships that run precisely as I wish them to run. In this case, we are speaking of a local friend, who I've known for some time. I met him when he was very young, brash, and edgy. Now he is... How do I put this? Something of a grumpy hermit who likes his village as it is. Sleepy. Undisturbed.*

Another wild swing of her drink, yet still no drop fell.

I informed him that this hotel was only going to grow in stature and desirability, and he could either fume about it, or get involved. He chose the latter.

You are very persuasive, Hannah had said.

Indeed I am, La Paloma had agreed, with a smile that might have appeared demure on someone else. On her it was nothing but an expression of power. *You will meet with him when he gets back from whatever trip he's currently on, doing whatever it is wealthy men do with their time.*

But she had laughed as if she knew very well what that was.

I told him you would explain the Christmas Jubilee that you have planned and walk him through the reservations, the festivities, and all the rest. I'm sure he will wish to put his stamp on things, as all men do, but I'm also certain that he will be deeply impressed with you.

The older woman had smiled then, wider than before,

and lifted her glass in Hannah's direction. *Because I am, you see, and I am not impressed by anything.*

It was only later, when she'd been cuddled up with Dominic and kissing his sweet head as he tried valiantly to fight off sleep, that it occurred to her that what Paloma had done was flatter her into acquiescence.

Not to mention a headache the following morning.

But now the day and the great man had arrived.

The whole hotel had been aflutter for two weeks. *Il maestro*, they had murmured, sometimes like prayers and sometimes like wild chants to the moon. *Il maestro sta arrivando qui!*

The master was coming here.

Hannah had no idea who *the master* was.

But she had learned early on in her career in hospitality that if she defaulted to her knee-jerk, Midwestern politeness, people made all kinds of assumptions about her. Mostly that they could treat her badly. So she had quickly developed a sleek, cool exterior. She'd learned how to do her blond hair in an icy sort of twist that sat at the nape of her neck, because she'd understood that elegance was a weapon when wielded correctly.

The more understated, the better.

She'd learned that walking in extremely high heels that looked as if they would break anyone else's ankles like twigs conveyed an air of authority that no flat shoe ever could, so she'd practiced in her tiny New York apartment until she could play basketball in her heels, if necessary.

And she'd learned that the people who responded best to all of this were the kind of overtly wealthy, wildly arrogant clientele used to getting their own way, who frequented five-star luxury hotels like this one.

She had also learned that while friendliness was never out of place, becoming *too* friendly with staff she might eventually have to fire hurt everyone, herself included. So Hannah did not sit down for any cozy chats with the rest of the staff about *il maestro*, whoever he was. Asking any of the staff who, exactly, this person was would be tantamount to admitting that she wasn't in control of every last detail in this hotel.

Hannah worked extremely hard to make it clear to everyone and anyone that she was more than in control.

That she was, in fact, the fuel that kept the whole place running smoothly.

This morning she walked inside the way she always did, in shoes that made other women wobble on the street. She pretended not to notice the way everyone scurried about at the sight of her. Everyone stood straighter, fixed their uniforms, and schooled their expressions to a pleasing blandness. She even saw one of the women behind the desk try to surreptitiously straighten one of the floral arrangements when it was already a symphony of vertical blossoming that needed no encouragement.

Hannah bit back a smile, inclined her head at everyone who caught her eye, and marched herself straight into her office. Inside, she had pictures only of the hotel, the hills, the glorious landscape stretched out in all directions.

No pictures of the baby. No pictures to indicate that she had any kind of personal life at all.

She had learned *that* lesson entirely too well in New York.

A glance at the slim gold watch on her wrist assured her that she still had time before the meeting. She was twenty minutes early, which was close enough to late for her. Hannah settled into her desk chair and fired up her desktop computer, then set about putting out a few fires that had blazed to life overnight.

But New York was in her head again. Hannah didn't like to think about New York. About how she trusted her friend, back when she'd had what passed for a social life in the hours she wasn't working at that restaurant. She had trusted her friend, she'd been indiscreet in what she'd thought was a safe space, and then she'd found her comments all over the news.

Manager of New York's favorite new hotspot doesn't like the food, they had all crowed.

It had been like a nightmare, but Hannah had never managed to wake up. Her phone had been filled with messages from all of her friends at work, wondering what on earth had possessed her. And from the obnoxious head chef himself, who had called her names she didn't like to think about, even all these years later.

She was surprised they hadn't fired her on the spot, but had instead forced her to work the busy weekend ahead. And she had only realized afterward that it had been a kind of exercise in public shame. Because every single person who had walked in that door that weekend had asked her if she was the one who'd been quoted, and when she'd said yes—because she might have been a fool but she wasn't a liar—had delivered a litany of hot takes on how wrong she was. Or had asked her to point out the parts of the extraordinarily expensive menu that were, in her own words, *up themselves*.

It would have been far preferable to have simply been fired on the spot.

Maybe she should have quit, but she'd held on to some slim thread of hope that *maybe*, if she showed that she was still the same hard worker she'd always been, they might rethink *one* indiscretion…

They had not.

And then on Sunday night, after her last shift—during which not one single person who worked at the restaurant would look her in the eye or speak to her directly—he had appeared.

By then she had accepted that she was getting fired. Because if she hadn't been, she was sure that she wouldn't have allowed the tall, almost brutally handsome man who'd watched her so intently from the bar to take her home.

She'd known that all the work she put into her life was about to be taken away from her. Worse, that it was her fault. She never should have trusted that she was in a safe space, not when the restaurant she worked at was the toast of New York.

It was the latest restaurant created by the billionaire restauranteur Antonluca. Once considered the greatest chef in the world, he had stopped cooking years ago and had turned his attention to a series of astonishingly good restaurants all over the world. He had even put together a series of television shows, none of which he appeared in, that had introduced an international audience not simply to his take on food but what many critics had dubbed the *Antonluca dining experience.*

Hannah had managed to be a part of all that, and had ruined it.

The man who'd turned up late and had watched her from the bar had seemed like an escape.

There was something about him. Stormy gray eyes. Close-cropped, inky black hair. He had been dressed in what should have been casual clothes—a button-down shirt thrown over trousers—but there was nothing casual about him. Maybe because it was clear at a glance that he was not American. American men never seemed so polished, nor so effortlessly beautiful. Even if it was his kind of beauty, that had seemed sharp at the edges.

The way she remembered it, she been drawn to him like he had her in some kind of tractor beam. Like she was helpless to resist.

You look unhappy, cara, he had said when she'd ventured near to pick up another silent order from the bartender she'd considered a friend, who had been acting as if she was a ghost.

What is happiness, really? she'd replied, realizing after she said it that it came out far more flirtatiously than she'd intended.

Maybe because she was so happy that *someone* was talking to her.

Something had shifted in that dark gray gaze of his. But if she'd expected him to flirt back at her, she was surprised. He had answered her question seriously.

To me, he had said, something intense in his gaze and all over his astonishingly perfect face, chiseled and *male* and beautiful, *happiness is never the goal. It is too often used to achieve things that cannot matter. Do you not think? When truly, it is joy or pain that we remember, in the end.*

He had said these things to her so intently. He had looked at her as if no other person existed in the world.

Looking back, was it any wonder that when he'd held out his hand, she put hers into his grasp without a second thought? It'd been a handshake, at first. When they'd still been in the restaurant.

Then, later, he had taken her in hand again. And he had taught her things that she still found herself dreaming about, all these years and his baby later.

She still didn't know his name.

But when they had fired her the next day, calling her into the restaurant and dismissing her, she'd taken it better than she might have otherwise. Because there was *him* to remember. There was that long, wildly hot night. She had lowered her eyes and had attempted to look meek and remorseful while the chef and Antonluca's business manager had decimated her.

Yet what she'd been thinking about was the way that beautiful man had moved inside of her. How he had kept her gasping and sobbing, trembling and begging, into the wee hours.

It had been like a balm.

Two months later, when she'd moved back to Nebraska because her name was poison in New York restaurant circles, it had been a bit less of a balm. Because she still didn't know his name. He hadn't given her that or his number or anything else. She wouldn't have the slightest idea how to go about finding him, even if she could call the restaurant and ask them to go through the receipts of that night—and she knew they wouldn't help her. Even if they might, she hadn't seen what he was drinking.

She'd thought it was a bit magical until then. She'd had this whole night out of time. A memory to tuck in her pocket and keep with her, something that was entirely hers and that no one else would ever have to know about.

Because, of course, she had not intended to get pregnant.

Then again, maybe things worked out the way they should, she thought as she checked her watch again and stood up. She set her computer to sleep, and picked up her folder once more. Because she now could not imagine a life without Dominic. Just as she couldn't imagine living anywhere but here. She had grown accustomed to Tuscan hills and cypress trees. And while her Italian was not fluent, it was getting there. She'd had her first dream in Italian a few months back and she loved *thinking* in a different language. Seeing and interpreting the world through the lens of a different vocabulary.

She also loved the small community she'd built here. She wasn't sure that she'd ever trust a friend again, but slowly, Cinzia had made inroads. Not that Hannah ever intended to repeat her error, but she did feel that since she trusted her landlady and neighbor with her child, she could probably also trust her with anything else.

After what had happened in New York, and that particular ex-friend's noted lack of remorse, that, too, felt like a balm.

So, too, did the hilltop village. There wasn't much to it. The *trattoria*. A tiny market. A handful of other shops that seemed open on a whim, if then. All arranged around the little square where there was a war memorial and the old men sat about and told lies about beautiful women they had known in their youth.

It was a sweet, good life. Hannah would raise her son here and Dominic would learn the good things in life first so that when he encountered the bad, he would have all this goodness built up ahead of time. Like armor.

All she had to do today was convince the new owner—the *maestro*—that she had everything in hand.

"Nervous?" asked the concierge, a fiercely French woman named Léontine, who was the closest thing that Hannah had to a friend at work. And who was also giving her French lessons twice a week, to expand Hannah's ability to interact with their international clientele.

If anyone else had asked her, she would have made it clear that the question was inappropriate. But this was Léontine, and Hannah could tell by the way she was asking it that she didn't think Hannah was nervous, nor should be. She was simply bracing. It was part of her charm.

"I'm not nervous at all," Hannah replied, which was true. She had always loved the art of pitching. She'd practiced it when she'd marched herself into this hotel, six months' pregnant and here on a tourist visa. If she wasn't good at selling herself, she wouldn't be any good at her job, which required that she sell the concept and fantasy of this hotel to everyone, including its owner. "But I'm used to La Paloma. I spent a long time learning how to handle her idiosyncrasies."

"Yes, but this is a man," Léontine said with a particularly French sort of shrug. "Whatever idiosyncrasies a man has, they are always...easily handled, in the end. Every woman must know this is so."

And Hannah wanted nothing more than to stand there and quiz her on what, precisely, she meant by that. But she couldn't, and not only because that would betray how very little experience Hannah had ever had with men. Something that she thought made her seem...odd, at best. And not in a good way. Odd in a way that led to pity, or worse, offers to set her up on dates she didn't want with men that she knew in advance she would dislike.

More pressingly, she could not risk being late. She smiled at her not-quite-friend and set off, marching through the grand lobby and making certain that everything was perfect as she passed. Every room was spacious, elegant, and set with windows that let Tuscany inside. At this time of year, the hotel was also sparkling and bright. Elegance gleamed from every direction. It was warm, inviting, suggesting Christmas without tipping over into the kind of raucous, American holiday displays that would be everywhere back home.

Suggestion was always more seductive than excess. Hannah had learned that in school and had seen it play out in each of her positions so far, though never so much as here.

Off the lobby, she made her way down the hallway that led to one of the hotel's restaurants, a few of its shops, and beyond it, what was known as the library.

She stepped inside at precisely eight o'clock. Extremely early by Italian standards, but she'd imagined that was part of the test.

Because no matter what La Paloma might have said about her position being secure, Hannah knew that this was a test.

She stepped inside, closing the door behind her, and was already letting her lips curve in polite greeting as she walked toward the figure of a man that she could see standing there by the window.

But he turned.

And she stopped dead.

She was fairly certain that her smile tumbled straight off of her lips and crashed down at her feet—but it could also have been her heart.

Because it was him.

Him.

Her mystery man from New York City.

Her balm during the hardest weekend of her life.

This beautiful, brutally attractive man, who had fully taken her hand. And had then taken her innocence, too, and had left her full of dreams of him for years after.

This man who had not given her his name, but had given her a far greater gift.

Her son.

And as his dark gray gaze locked on to hers, then widened in dark, arrogant astonishment, something else occurred to her.

This man was *the father of her son*. And he didn't know it. He couldn't.

And unless she was wildly mistaken, or in the wrong meeting room, he was also the new owner of this hotel.

Which meant that the life Hannah had built so carefully, and loved so much, was about to come tumbling down.

Again.

CHAPTER TWO

Antonluca Aniello could not believe his eyes.

Hannah Hansen—*the* Hannah Hansen—stood before him, somehow even more beautiful than he remembered her.

As if she gleamed in a new way, here in Italy where beauty was a passion, a lifelong journey, a way of life.

There were a lot of women named Hannah Hansen in the world. Antonluca knew this too well. So while he had noted the name when given her details during the sale, he hadn't thought anything of it. Or rather, he knew better by now, because he'd looked for her to no avail.

For years.

Because he had been haunted by that night in New York.

More haunted than he should have been, or could even accept for some months afterward, since the entire reason he'd met her in the first place was because he'd been *incensed* by that idiotic thing she'd said.

And worse, had shared with the whole world in a dirty tabloid rag.

He could still remember all of it as if it had been

yesterday, especially now that she stood before him as if frozen in place, just as he was. His mind spun out the way it had the first time he'd seen those green eyes of hers, reminding him of the only peace he'd ever known—the land he'd bought in these very same hills.

Back then he'd been in Japan, minding his own business and going about his life, overseeing a new restaurant build. Until his phone had blown up, with everyone he knew rushing to tell him that there was a snake in the grass at his New York restaurant.

That the manager of the restaurant—a position that should have come with some level of decorum and discretion to accompany the excellent pay—had shot her mouth off to some tabloid reporter.

If you like fancy, it's fine, the woman had said, according to the papers. *But it's an* experience. *It's not a meal. I eat before I go to work and sometimes grab a snack on the way home, too.*

The *audacity*. The astonishing *cheek* of it, to take his money and then turn around and talk about him this way, as if his Michelin stars were meaningless. As if being named the most exciting thing to happen to the culinary arts in a generation was nothing more than lip service.

She *grabbed a snack* on the way home from work? Antonluca had been incensed. Dangerously so.

He had managed over the years to tamp down on the wildfire temper that some people—including himself, back in his early days—called *passion* and *artistic tem-*

perament. When Antonluca was entirely too aware that whatever it was, wherever it came from, it made him act like one of those stereotypical chefs. Forever barking out terse orders in a busy kitchen, having temper tantrums over side dishes and meltdowns regarding the temperature of the soup.

All things worthy of having tantrums over, to his mind. But there was no denying that there was a certain point at which the tantrum became a sideshow, drawing attention away from the reason they were all there in the first place: the food.

His food.

She's gone, his business manager had assured him when Antonluca had taken his call. *I'll fire her myself.*

I think not, Antonluca had replied, glaring out at the dark Tokyo night on the other side of his hotel penthouse window, his voice scathing. *I think I will come to New York myself and see if I find my food more of an amusement park ride than a meal. Perhaps this woman is correct. If so, she deserves a raise.*

And so he had stormed onto his waiting jet and fumed his way across the planet.

Somewhere high in the air, he accepted the unpleasant fact that he wouldn't have been so outraged if he wasn't concerned that there was *some* truth in what she'd said. Cruising along at high altitude, he had been forced to face something he'd known that he'd been avoiding for a while.

The truth was simple and devastating. He, Antonluca

Aniello, who had *redefined Italian cuisine*—according to everyone—did not feel connected to his food any longer. Not in the way he had been, way back when he'd started.

Back when he'd accidentally found his way into a restaurant in Rome and had saved his own life. And not only his.

He had started off washing dishes. He had been thirteen and big for his age, so it had been easy enough to pretend he was older. And working in that kitchen had been a means to an end, at first. It had meant money, and that had been all he'd cared about. Because money meant that he could take care of his siblings—and keep them from making far more desperate choices out on the streets of Rome.

Bad things happened to homeless children, as Antonluca knew all too well.

And he was the oldest, so it fell to him to figure out a solution.

So he had. He'd worked his way up from washing dishes to cutting up vegetables, and then had picked up more than that as he went along. He'd slowly become fluent in the language of food. The dance of flavor, the subtle language of texture, the magic of presentation.

The restaurant had been a family affair, unpretentious and casual and, after a while, welcoming. Antonluca's interests had been encouraged. Emiliano, the owner and cook, had taught Antonluca everything that he knew—until Antonluca was cooking the dinner service himself.

Soon after that, he began tinkering with the dishes and playing around with the restaurant offerings. And when the day came that he took over for the man who had become more or less the only father he'd ever known, Antonluca had turned it into one of the finest restaurants in Rome.

To this day, people still traveled from all over the world to stand in line on a narrow Roman street—because he refused to take reservations—simply to eat at the few small tables where he had started.

If he really stopped to think about it all, it was astonishing. Still. To have come from so little and to be where he was now, buying hotels on a whim.

But he remembered how that had happened, too, he thought, as he and Hannah still stood frozen in that same moment while these things flashed through his head. Because he had still been responsible for his siblings, he'd branched out from Emiliano's. He'd worked so he could give each one of his siblings half ownership in a restaurant, to make sure that all of them would be taken care of forever.

The way his mother would have wanted, if she'd been in her right mind instead of addled on drugs. If she'd lived.

The restaurant business was volatile, but Antonluca's take on elevated staples never seemed to go out of style. And when he had restaurants all over Europe, and a few in the United States, he didn't stop. Because his younger brothers and sisters were messy and complicated and he was the only one who could help. He was the only one who understood.

So he did what he could.

But somewhere in there, he'd stopped experimenting in the kitchen.

While he was busy building an empire, he'd retreated into the boardrooms, he'd taken the meetings, and he'd told himself it was because he was retreating from the celebrity he'd never wanted as fast as he could.

He'd told himself that the food spoke for itself.

Trust some brash, reckless American to call all that into question.

Because if his food had no soul, then neither did Antonluca.

He had gone to New York to find out, once and for all.

What he had discovered instead was Hannah.

Hannah with her golden hair, her eyes like emerald fields, and her total trust in him. Hannah, who had somehow humbled the man who had once been called so arrogant that he circled back around to charming.

Maybe because he had known, even if she hadn't, that she shouldn't have trusted him at all. That he bore her significant ill will, confused though that had become once he touched her and felt that unmistakable fire blaze to life between them.

He had thought, *Absolutely not.*

But he had done it anyway.

Because he could hardly bring himself to recall why

it was he should treat her as anything but a revelation when he got lost in all that green and gold.

Yet even now, blindsided by a woman he had convinced himself could not be *his* Hannah Hansen, Antonluca did not regret that night.

How could he, when he could not recall a single day that had passed since that he had not remembered some part of it in minute detail?

Now, standing in this library that had been spruced up considerably since he'd known it as a younger man, when he'd visited Paloma and one of her husbands here—to cook for them, though that was not the story the Paloma liked to tell, as if there was some world where a street kid from Rome and one of the most famous socialites in Europe would interact otherwise— he watched as Hannah's perfect face…reddened. He watched her green eyes go wide.

She looked very much as if she'd seen a ghost, and he found some kind of solace in that. Because, clearly, she hadn't been anticipating running into him today, either. He found that there were a thousand questions he needed to ask her.

Only some of them involving the running of Paloma's pet hotel.

But they were alone in this room. And the last time they had been alone together, they'd both been naked, tangled around each other as the morning light streamed into the hotel he'd taken her to. He'd meant to leave her several times before he'd actually managed to do it. And so his last memory of her was her sprawled out on the bed they'd torn apart, a smile on her face and that lush body he had come to know so well over the course of that long night limp and boneless.

He could probably paint that image, so perfect was his memory of it, if he possessed even the slightest bit of talent in that area.

Her lips parted as if she meant to say something, or was trying to say something, but no sound emerged.

Antonluca moved closer to her, and this was a different time. A different country. This was *his* country and if he hadn't been standing here in front of her, watching her react to the sight of him, he would have been certain that she'd set this up somehow. That she'd gone to the trouble of anticipating Paloma's whims—a risky proposition at best—and had then inserted herself into the project, hoping that it would one day throw her into his path.

He would have been certain of it because he already knew that people went to great lengths to insinuate themselves with him. It was one of the major reasons that he had more or less cut himself off from anyone he hadn't known for years upon years. Because he could no longer trust the motivations of people who appeared out of nowhere. He could never be certain if they wanted to know *him* or his empire.

But Hannah did not look triumphant. She looked shaken to her core.

And before he knew it, he was standing before her, close enough to touch.

She was wearing those heels again, the ones that he remembered vividly from New York. She had charged down the street in them as if they were flats. More importantly, they had made her tall enough so that all she had to do was tilt her head back, just a little, to look him in the face.

When he was not a small man.

Antonluca had worked hard for the whole of his life to strip himself of the recklessness and rashness that had plagued his family since before he was born, if what he recalled of his mother's stories was true. Cooking had saved him. Cooking was the art of marrying precision with process, and he'd been good at that. He'd *excelled* at it. And running a kitchen involved intense focus and control not only of himself, but of others, and he'd excelled at that, too.

In these last years, he had decided that what he needed most of all was peace. No carrying on in kitchens. No drama, no concerns about the fakeness of the people around him, no need to worry about who wanted to cozy up to him or worse, one of his more vulnerable siblings.

If he retreated to Tuscany, which had always seemed to him—a street kid from the grand old mess of a city that was Rome—as a beacon of hope and tranquility, he was sure that he could find it.

But she had shattered any hope of finding peace three years ago.

So Antonluca shattered it further now by moving closer still, sliding his hand along her jaw as if he had the right, then drawing her closer so he could settle his mouth to hers.

It felt like burning himself alive, beautifully.

It felt like coming home.

But he pushed that concerning notion aside, because their mouths fit together perfectly. Still. And the heat between them was still there, instant and overwhelming and *perfect*.

Antonluca was a connoisseur of flavor and hers had no equal.

He licked his way into her mouth and then enjoyed that slick, hot, connection. The way she kissed him back immediately, as if she had hungered for him in precisely this way, the same way he had for her.

Across time. Across the sea.

The kiss deepened, got darker and richer.

He remembered this, too. The way this fire danced inside of him, lighting him up, making his cock hard at once, as if he'd never touched anyone but her. Nor ever would.

He remembered the way she had gifted him her innocence with that smile of hers, shy but bold at the same time, and how he had thought to himself then that he would do anything at all to make sure that every memory she had of that night was a good one.

Even though this was the woman who had betrayed him in the press.

Something that hadn't changed in all these intervening years, now that he thought about it.

And maybe she was having second thoughts herself, because she pushed away then. She stepped back to put space between them, her fingers rising to press against her lips.

Once again, they stared at each other as the cold December morning beamed in from outside.

Hannah dropped her hand and he watched as she put her armor back in place. When he kissed her, she was supple and pliable in his arms, but as he stood there she…became someone else.

Cool. Remote. Formidable, even.

But she was still Hannah. He could see it in her eyes.

Those beautiful green eyes that reminded him of summer.

"I don't even know your name," she said.

This, Antonluca found difficult to comprehend. "Of course you must know my name. Or did you think you were meeting with a ghost?"

Her green eyes narrowed slightly. This, he discovered, made her no less beautiful. Not even when her lovely chin lifted in what could only be called a quiet act of aggression. "You are only known in these parts as *il maestro*, I fear."

Antonluca would not have believed anyone else who said such a thing to him, but this was Hannah.

Because he knew that she had not recognized him that night in New York.

But surely she must have figured out who he was since. He thought it was unlikely that his business manager wouldn't have mentioned that it had been Antonluca himself at the restaurant at night, though he might not have known what had happened afterward.

Now, as then, she looked at him so guilelessly that he simply couldn't believe that she would lie. Or that she *could*.

When, truly, he should have known by now that everyone lied, and especially to him if they thought they might benefit from it in some way.

He almost wanted to remain a mystery to her forever, because he couldn't remember the last time someone hadn't known who he was on sight. He *almost* wanted to keep this revelation going for as long as it could.

But something in him wanted her to *know him* more.

So he told her, straight and almost harsh. "I am Antonluca Aniello, Hannah."

And then he watched her turn so pale he thought for a moment that she might collapse. He even moved slightly forward, prepared to catch her, but she didn't swoon. Or crumple at his feet. She stood very still for a very long time, swayed only slightly, and then turned away from him, moving back across the library floor.

He thought she might actually walk out—but it seemed she was pacing, because she turned around again, and marched back to him in the same agitated fashion.

"You," she said as if she could not comprehend it. As if it didn't make sense. "*You* are Antonluca. *The* Antonluca."

He inclined his head. "I am."

He said no more than that. And he watched, fascinated, as a deep, bright color shot back into her cheeks.

"That's why you came to New York." Her gaze was wider now, and slicked with something he couldn't quite identify. "You weren't a random stranger at the bar, a beautiful escape from the worst weekend of my life. You were there because of that article." She swallowed as if it hurt. "Was this your plan all along? To…to…*punish* me for what I said to my…"

She couldn't say it, but she didn't have to say it. He was appalled all the same.

He shook his head, emphatically. "I came to confront you and had no intention of doing anything more than that."

"But you did." Her green gaze never left his face. "You did far more than that."

Once again, Antonluca felt the stirrings of his temper that, apparently, only she could produce in him.

"By all means," he gritted out. "Let's interrogate what happened between us that night, but we must not forget that the reason I was there in the first place was because you, the manager of my restaurant, disparaged my food. If there is a more perfect example of biting the hand that feeds, I do not know what it is."

"I had a conversation with a friend," Hannah said, as

if she had wanted to say this for a long time. As if the words were coming of their own accord. "A friend I'd had many private conversations with before. It never occurred to me in a million years that she would take that conversation and *publish* it." Her eyes were accusing again, but not, he thought, aimed at him this time. "She betrayed me. And I expected to get fired, of course. I'm not justifying what I said, or pretending that you didn't have every right to be furious."

"I thank you, *cara*, for your permission."

She glared at him and that bone-dry tone of his, and all he could think about was that he had messed up her lip gloss. He wanted to mess it up even further.

Which did not exactly make it easy to access the fury he had felt when he'd flown across the planet to upbraid her three years ago.

"I take full responsibility for the indiscretion," she said then, in a cool sort of way that managed to lodge itself directly under his skin. "That is what I told everyone involved back then. And would have told you, too, had you mustered up the courage to tell me who you were."

"It was not a matter of courage," he retorted. "It was self-preservation."

"Yes, of course. Because a famous billionaire needs protection from a no-name restaurant worker. That's how the world works."

"Hannah." And even from between his teeth, he liked her name in his mouth. "I did not take advantage of you. I expected to sit down at a table and have a discussion with you. Probably not a pleasant one. I did not anticipate what happened."

And Antonluca knew that she remembered it. He could see it. He knew that she'd been as shocked as he was that a simple brush of hands could change everything so profoundly, but it had.

It had changed *him*, and he hated it.

"It seems as if you found an excellent way to take revenge on me," she replied, her green eyes dark. "I suppose I should congratulate you."

He moved in closer then, and ran his thumb over her lips. Those full, sensual lips that he craved another taste of, even now.

"Be honest," he said in a low voice that he could hardly credit as his own. "Did anything that happened that night feel like revenge to you?"

Hannah flushed and took a step back. She crossed her arms, looking very much as if she was gathering herself. He took that as a compliment, for that would not be required if she wasn't as off balanced by this he was.

Not that he intended to let her know that.

"I suppose none of this matters," she said after what felt like a very, very long moment. "You didn't expect to see me, nor I you. But the fact remains, we will need to work together." She inclined her head. "I understand that the hotel is now yours. And as certainly as there can only be one La Paloma, things will surely change under your leadership. I hope you find me flexible, committed, and excited to dig in."

It was that armor again, Antonluca thought. He did not care for it.

But by the same token, her head was clearly cooler than his. Or she was better at pretending. He reminded himself, as he always did in business situations, that he had the upper hand.

Because most people in business did not come from backgrounds like his. He had read Hannah's résumé when he'd flown back from Japan and he never forgot the things he read. He knew that she'd had a pleasantly middle-class life, had gone to university, and while she might not have grown up as privileged as some, she had certainly had advantages that he had not.

It was a superpower, he sometimes thought. He saw through people in ways that others couldn't, because his very survival—and that of his siblings—had depended on him being able to read people in an instant.

It was one of the reasons the magnificent Paloma herself liked him so much. He always told the truth, like it or not.

"Do you believe that we can have an appropriate working relationship?" he asked her, drawing his own armor close.

She frowned at him. "I have never had anything but appropriate working relationships before. I don't think that I have a problem."

"You were just kissing me as if your life depended upon it."

She frowned harder, but there was that color on her

cheeks, and it deepened. "I think you're confusing you for me."

"The truth is that I'm not a Puritan in the way you Americans tend to be," he told her, and shrugged in a way he knew was deeply Italian. "I do not necessarily feel the need to divorce the personal from other parts of my life."

"Why are you talking about this as if we were planning an affair?" she asked, her eyes narrowing—but again, the color on her cheeks told a different tale. "We have a Christmas Jubilee to put on. We have to convince some of the wealthiest, most jaded people on the planet to believe in wonder. To feel at peace. To surrender to an idea of Christmas when they could literally go anywhere or do anything else."

That hit him harder than it should have. It made him almost wish—

But he shoved that aside.

"I'm not sure I'm being the unrealistic one in this scenario," he said instead, darker than he'd intended. "I have already had you fired from one job, Hannah. What makes you think that this one will go more smoothly?"

"The village is very small," she retorted. "Not a lot of paparazzi hanging about. Somehow I think I'll manage to keep my disparaging remarks to myself."

He only studied her, taking stock of the things that were happening inside of him. The way his heart was beating too fast. The way his body was reacting to being in her presence. The heavy ache in his cock, the taste of her in his mouth.

This was all a terrible idea.

But then, he had already thought it was a bad idea when Paloma had approached him and he'd had no idea that Hannah was involved. Here he was anyway.

You have the opportunity to belong to something, the old woman had said. *Instead of simply wasting into nothing in this privacy of yours, hermetically sealed away from the rest of the world.*

I like being alone, he had replied.

If that were true, my dear boy, Paloma had said with a laugh, *you would be happy.*

And Antonluca had told her in no uncertain terms that he had never been happier in his life. But he understood now, standing in this library, that he had lied.

He hadn't meant to. But now, with Hannah here before him, he understood that there was a difference between living as he had been and *feeling alive*, which was how he felt in her presence.

Like it or not.

He wanted to put his hands on her. He wanted to pull her into his arms again, and kiss her senseless.

He wanted that to only be the beginning.

But perhaps there was something to be said for enjoying these feelings. They were so new. So different. They reminded him of how he'd felt years ago when he'd first started creating his poetry with food, creating dishes out of dreams, and feeling so connected to the particular joy of the meal well-made.

He hadn't believed that he would ever feel that way again.

Antonluca did not pull her into his arms. Instead, he crossed over to the table in the center of the library floor, pulled out a chair, and sat down. She looked at him warily as he waved his hand at the seat opposite his.

"I'm certain we will find a way to work together, Hannah," he said. "After all, you have already proven that we can get along beautifully when you please. Why should this be any different? Let Christmas bells ring."

And he waited, not certain what she would do, as she stood there frowning at him.

But when she came over to the table and sat down with him, he allowed himself a smile.

CHAPTER THREE

HANNAH EXPECTED FIREWORKS, high drama, and soap opera scenes at every turn, as befit the kind of chef Antonluca had been when he'd spent all his time in his kitchens.

But there was none of that. Not the faintest hint of it from Antonluca when, if she didn't police herself appropriately, she could still taste that mouth of his on hers.

And, frankly, even when she tried to police herself, for that matter.

She had to grapple with why she found that a little too close to disappointing. So close, in fact, that every evening when she drove home through the sleepy village she had to interrogate herself over every last moment of their interactions because she was terribly afraid that *she* was the one who wasn't quite maintaining the right level of professionalism.

It was galling. Especially because she had already proved to him how unprofessional she was in New York.

Twice, not that she was counting.

Over the next week, she met with Antonluca every day. They went over every part of the hotel and how it did business, and she found herself impressed with him despite very much wanting that not to be the case.

When it came to business, Antonluca was focused, engaged, and very, very smart.

She had somehow convinced herself that he wouldn't be. That he *couldn't* be.

That had been the gossip around the kitchen in New York. That, sure, once upon a time the man had been able to cook a decent dinner after a fashion, but that it was a bit of savvy marketing that had made him a name. All smoke and mirrors and excellent branding.

He's basically a chain at this point, the restaurant's chef had said once, though naturally without those remarks turning up in the tabloids. *People trust the name. The food is secondary.*

That counted as a sick burn in the kitchens of Manhattan.

But what Hannah learned during her time with him at La Paloma was that nothing was *secondary* to Antonluca Aniello. He was interested in *everything*. No detail was too small. No topic was off-limits.

Sitting with him each day, she found that he asked all the right questions, and many that she would not have thought to ask herself. And as she watched him learn the ins and outs of the hotel in real time—and quicker than she had, if she was brutally honest—she could only be impressed with the way his mind worked.

By the end of that first week it seemed very unlikely to her that anyone but Antonluca had been responsible for his meteoric rise. And really, there was something satisfying about that. At least he'd earned his position in life. There was nothing worse than someone who acted like they'd earned it, but hadn't.

She found that she was okay with Antonluca's business acumen—and the fame it had garnered him—now that she'd seen it in action. It made sense that he was as huge as he was. That was something close enough to comforting, really. How sad would it have been if she'd thought the opposite?

The business part of things was going swimmingly, Hannah thought.

It was that personal spark between them that she couldn't quite get a handle on.

"How is it possible you did not know who I was?" he asked one day as they sat there, going over various spreadsheets and graphs. When she looked at him, he raised one of those dark, slashing brows of his and she felt everything inside her…flutter. "My face has been plastered across all of my various properties for years. It is inescapable."

He did not say that as if he liked it.

But Hannah focused on the question he'd asked. It was that or the *fluttering*, and she thought it would be better all around if she ignored that.

"It has," she agreed. She sat back in her chair, aware that she was sitting entirely too close to him and if she only leaned in— *Stop that right now*, she ordered herself. "But it wasn't *this* face, was it?" She waved her hand at him when his brow rose higher. "First of all, the iconic image of Antonluca, celebrity chef, has you laughing. There's some facial hair. The actual hair on your head is significantly longer."

He gazed at her without comprehension.

Hannah sighed. "I'm afraid you look absolutely nothing like your picture."

That clearly did not sit well with him. "I beg your pardon?"

"The man I met in the bar was intense. That whole night was intense." That was an error, she realized, when the dark gray blaze of his gaze seemed to work its way inside her, connecting to that *flutter* and making it... something else entirely. She hurried on. "I'm not sure I have ever seen you smile. Much less *laugh*. And I'll be honest with you." Now it was like she was skidding down some icy hill in winter with no hope of stopping herself, so she didn't. Maybe she couldn't. "For some reason, that picture of you always made me think you were short."

He made a strangled sort of noise. "Short? *Me?*"

In fairness, that was likely greatly surprising indeed to a man who looked to be comfortably over six feet and three inches even while sitting. And better resembled a gloriously urbane giant when he was standing. And that wasn't even getting into the things he could do when he was lying—

But really, she lectured herself. *You must stop this.*

"No one in the restaurant had ever met you personally," she said. "Except the chef, I think, but it's not as if *he* spent any time talking to the rest of us." She shook her head, those chaotic, high-energy days bright in her memory for a moment. She both missed them and wouldn't return to them for all the money in the world, even if she could. "There is no reason whatsoever that I should have thought that *Antonluca himself* would descend upon me that night. Then, afterward, I had other things to think about than one long night in New York City."

Once again, she only realized the moment she said that sort of thing that she shouldn't have. It only encouraged the heat between them to thicken, to feel even more dangerous all around them when this was a professional meeting. They were sitting in her office, a place she had made certain offered no hint about her private life.

Because she had learned, hadn't she? If she behaved like a person, people treated her like one. If she acted like an impenetrable veneer of a person instead, they were too afraid of her to do anything.

She had learned, but now Antonluca was here and there was all that *fluttering* and there was something in his gray gaze that made her think he knew it. That he could feel it, too.

Hannah decided she really didn't want to wait to hear his reply. "I was fired, after all. And there was no getting a new job, not in New York. Or not in any New York restaurants, anyway." She risked another look at him then, hoping the temperature had gone down somewhat. But his gray eyes were as hot and intense on hers as ever. She swallowed hard, and looked away again. "I spent a few weeks denying reality and then I had to move out of my apartment before I bankrupted myself. I headed back to Nebraska. Not what I wanted, but I thought it was a good place to regroup and figure out my next move."

"And was it?"

Hannah knew that this was an opportunity to tell him about Dominic. This was not only *an opportunity*—she was already well overdue for that particular confession. It should have been the first thing out of her mouth the minute she'd seen him. She shouldn't have allowed a single sentence or moment or whole *kiss* to go by without sharing the news that he was a parent.

She still didn't know why she hadn't done it. Why she hadn't simply told him the way she'd always been certain she would, when she had imagined running into that gloriously decadent stranger again.

But even as she thought that, here in her office where the air between them seemed absurdly charged, she knew it was a lie. She knew why she hadn't told him then. And why she hadn't made up for that oversight since. She was afraid.

It was as simple as that. She was afraid that telling him about Dominic would fundamentally change the life she'd made here, probably forever. It was highly likely that it would be ruined altogether because there were so many ways he could react—and most of them were negative. This was a man who had come to confront her in person because he didn't like stupid things she'd said to a third party. Look how *that* had ended.

The truth was that she'd thought it was entirely too possible that letting him in on Dominic's existence would be as life-altering as letting him into *her* life had been back then. And the trouble with life-altering events, she'd decided, was that it was impossible to tell how and where that alteration would occur. How it would really mess everything up.

Hannah had been afraid. She was still afraid.

Maybe even more afraid than before, because now she couldn't tell herself that this man was a momentary madness and nothing else. She couldn't assure herself that if she ever ran into him again, she would feel nothing and might even laugh that she'd ever felt so *drawn* to him.

There was no comforting herself with that fantasy any longer.

She stared at him for what felt like an eternity, then she made herself look back down at her tidy spreadsheets and careful graphs, where there was only data. Nothing to fear at all.

"Nebraska is always a good place to land," she told him when she was certain she could keep her voice even. "It's always nice to be back home. It allows me to really think about how to make the next move, and where I want to go."

Which was, she thought, a very diplomatic way of saying that being at home in the little town where she'd grown up, surrounded by her prickly family members, was an excellent way to force a person into making *absolutely sure* that she could get out again. Because Hannah had decided long ago, when she was all of ten and obsessed with Amelia Earhart, that she had no intention of staying there.

And even if she'd had the *intention* of staying there, it wasn't as if anyone in the house she'd grown up in was at all welcoming. So. It had all worked itself out, in the end.

But she didn't tell him that. Just like she didn't tell him about Dominic—again.

She focused on the data and told herself she would do the right thing *eventually*. When the time was right.

Hannah was sure she would know when that was.

Another week passed, and the Tuscan hills got even colder. Hannah moved on from sitting in too-close rooms talking about data and the hotel to having Antonluca shadow her as she moved through her day, the better to get a more dynamic sense of what happened at the hotel at any given moment.

He had requested immersion, apparently, and that was what he was getting.

And while Hannah was initially delighted not to be in such close quarters with him for hours each day, she quickly realized that this part of his long introduction to La Paloma was almost more of a challenge. Seeing the man in motion made her…too aware of him.

Much too aware of him.

"I'm surprised you don't already have a hotel," she said one day. "Or a whole host of them."

"I like food." His dark gaze moved over her face in that way he had, that made her want to make wishes for things she knew better than to want. "I've always preferred restaurants over hotels."

But he was saying this while they were finishing a sweep of the hotel's restaurants, the three of them ranging from casually elegant to downright lavish. Hannah found herself studying his face, trying to read his expressions, doing her best to figure out what he thought about the various offerings. About the decor. About the entrées he could see served before him. About the service itself.

About...*everything*.

She was also aware that it didn't really help that all the servers knew precisely who he was and were acting—by which she meant *overacting*—accordingly.

"You will be able to make all the hotel's restaurants in your image as well," she said, cheerfully, because it felt like the worst kind of surrender to *show* how nervous she was around him. Because that was what it was, she was certain. Simple *nerves*. Not *fluttering*, just nerves being nervy, or whatever it was nerves did. "They have always been rated consistently high across the board, but that is not in the same stratosphere as an Antonluca property, of course."

It seemed to her that it took him a forebodingly long

time to turn and look down at her, his expression finally readable.

And it was sheer arrogance.

"Yet my understanding is that they eat meals here, rather than have circus-like experiences."

Hannah felt herself flush. She smiled at the maître d' as they passed, then marched her way out, wishing fervently that she was not so keenly aware of how closely Antonluca followed behind her. Once they were outside, she fought her own body not to indicate that she was cold. Because this particular restaurant, the fanciest of their three offerings, stood in its own building on the hilltop and the wind this evening felt like knives.

But she faced him anyway and pretended she was warm.

"You are still holding on to that," she observed, trying her best to sound...well. Something close enough to amused. "All these years later."

She expected him to deny that. Then bluster on the way men often did, pretending they had no feelings about anything.

But Antonluca was an Italian man. He did nothing of the kind.

"But of course I am still holding on to it," he replied at once, and not as if he was remotely amused. "You essentially called my life's work a sideshow. A *circus*, Hannah. What reaction did you expect me to have?"

"I ate in your restaurant in Florence," she told him. He scowled at her, so she tipped her chin up and folded her arms, which had the added benefit of making her feel slightly warmer, too. "I believe it was one of the earlier ones in your portfolio."

"It was my second restaurant," he said coolly. "But the first one I opened myself."

"Like your flagship restaurant in Rome, it is a small, cozy, neighborhood sort of place."

"You sound like Wikipedia."

"That was actually written on the menu in Florence," Hannah acknowledged. "But do you want to know what I think?"

"It seems as if you plan to tell me." His voice was a dark thread of menace, somehow colder and hotter than the December wind, all at once. "Whether I wish to hear it or not."

"It made me understand why you're so famous," Hannah told him quietly. She had waited in line outside for over an hour and a half and had sat at a tiny table crammed in between two larger, more boisterous parties. She'd ordered three things. A salad, a plate of pasta, and a single cannoli. And every single bite had been *transformative*. "It wasn't an art installation on a plate. It was a meal. Possibly one of the best meals I've ever had."

"An *art installation*," he repeated, in disbelief. Those gray eyes of his blazed at her. "*An art installation on a plate.*"

"I'm just telling you my impression."

"And here I thought you wanted to keep your job."

Hannah supposed that she should have been intimidated by that, but she wasn't. If anything, it was a relief. It reminded her of the stakes here. It reminded her of exactly who they were, and what that meant.

Yes, there were things she should tell him. But also, yes—he was a powerful man who could fire her once again, and then what would she do? How would that help Dominic?

She really should have thanked him.

"I do want my job," she told him, after a moment, because she had to breathe first. "But in order to keep it, I suspect that you will need to know that you can trust me. If not me, personally, than certainly that I will tell you the truth." She considered that obvious, glaring falsehood and added, "I am always scrupulously direct when it comes to my opinions, especially at work. You can depend on that. You'll notice that I never apologized for what I felt about your food in New York. Only for the indiscretion in talking about it to someone who was not, as it turned out, a friend, after all."

He shook his head at that and had the look of someone who might have laughed, if they were the laughing kind. If he was actually the picture they trotted out and claimed was him. "You think this is a mark in your favor, do you?"

"I do." When his storm-tossed eyes slammed into her, she managed to shrug. "You are a very wealthy man. I'm sure you have more yes-men than you know what to do with. La Paloma liked the fact that this is not a role I know how to play."

"Neither does Paloma herself," he muttered.

It did occur to her then that they were standing here, outside a restaurant, in weather cold enough to keep everyone else safely and firmly indoors. There were no staff, no guests, anywhere nearby. They were as close to alone as it was possible to be in a fully booked-out hotel.

Something she couldn't stop thinking about, feverishly, when he stepped toward her as if he was about to—

But he didn't do it. He didn't put his hands on her. He didn't lean in any closer. He didn't so much as graze her with a stray finger, yet her entire body reacted as if he'd plugged her directly into an electrical outlet, like one of the bare trees strung with lights around them.

Worse than that, since she was standing here in the cold with nothing resembling a coat, she was fairly certain that he could see every last reaction her body had to all those things he *didn't* do.

Something simmered, there in that dark gaze of his. She thought she saw something awfully close to triumph, but then he stepped away again. And the spell was broken.

Hannah told herself she was relieved.

"I'll take that under advisement," he growled at her, and then set off for the main building at a pace that had her very nearly running to keep up.

And later, at home, after she'd settled Dominic into bed, she found she dreamed up a hundred different endings to that interaction. All of them involving his mouth on hers, or other tender parts of her body.

That was the trouble. She remembered entirely too well what it was like to lose herself in him. She remembered the particular wildfire of his touch and the way he seemed to read and understand every single one of her body's responses.

Alone in bed in her cottage, snuggled down deep beneath the covers, she shivered. She *fluttered*.

More than once.

And then, as the days grew shorter and darker still, the real holiday bustle began. Hannah had to trade in her intimidating heels for boots that she could wear to trample over the field at the base of the hill where they were setting up the hotel's own Christmas market. It was this part of their so-called Christmas Jubilee that Hannah was the most proud. She had pitched it to La Paloma herself, having been so entranced by the winter markets all over Europe—particularly in Florence—and was sure that the hotel could do something exciting.

She was overseeing the setting up of the many booths on the morning the market began, happily wearing layers against the cold, when she became aware of that same brooding presence, right there at her shoulder.

"I have never understood the appeal of a Christmas market," Antonluca told her flatly when she looked over at him.

"I don't think that it's the sort of thing that can be explained," Hannah replied mildly. She nodded at one of her vendors, and tried to unobtrusively herd Antonluca away before he offended everyone. "You either think it's delightful or you don't."

When she looked at him then, he was staring around at all the different stands festooned with Christmas colors and piled high with holiday wares. And not as if he was in the least bit delighted by what he saw.

"Let me guess," she said with a sigh that she told herself was amused. "This is not your favorite time of year."

He seemed to take his time looking back at her and she swore that there was something almost...*guarded* in his gaze then. "I prefer to work through Christmas. And every other holiday. People need to eat, and in any case, I have never felt the urge to...reach out to assorted angels or proclaim good news to anyone."

But he said this so gruffly that it made something in her ache. More than it should have.

"Christmas was the one day a year where everyone pretended to get along," Hannah told him softly, running her fingers over evergreen boughs piled high on a table as they passed. "It was the one day a year where I could pretend that everything was the way it ought to have been. It always felt magical."

"What is magical about pretending that something is other than what it is?" he asked. Tersely, she thought.

"It's better than nothing, I think. Isn't it?"

They had stopped walking at some point, and while Hannah was dimly aware of all the workmen and vendors rushing around them, all she could really focus on was Antonluca. He looked like something out of one of those dreams she liked to have, alone in her cozy bed. He wore a dark wool coat and a silk scarf and he was so beautiful that she was tempted to tell him that he need only believe in the archangel he found in his mirror—

But that was a bit fanciful, even for her.

"It's perfectly all right if you don't like Christmas," she told him. "But between holiday pricing and our expectations of profit from the Christmas Market, not to mention the other events we have planned throughout the rest of this month, the hotel will make enough that it could close for the rest of the year if it wished. We will have to see in January if my projections are correct, but look around." It almost hurt then, to pull her gaze from his and to gesture about at the commotion on all sides. "Everyone else is thrilled."

She expected him to bark something back at her, but he didn't. Once again, he surprised her. He really did look around, that dark, restless gaze of his moving this way and that.

Taking it all in, she thought. Adding it all up in that ledger in his head, pluses and minuses. Or, anyway, that was how she assumed wealthy men thought about the world when, for all she knew, *this* wildly rich man was hanging around for vibes only.

Something she did not intend to say to him.

When his gaze returned to her it seemed darker, somehow. "I assume your projections will be correct.

It's one of the reasons why my restaurants have always stayed open on Christmas Day. Profit is hand over fist."

And he had made such a point of telling her he wasn't American. Or *puritan*, as he had put it. She had to take that to mean that there were different boundaries here.

So she asked him a question she would not have asked the forbidding La Paloma. Not without second-guessing herself, that was. "What are some of the other reasons?"

She thought he looked taken back, which was a kind of victory in itself. He let out a sound that might have been a laugh, though it sounded far too bitter.

"My mother usually made certain that she was completely out of her mind on Christmas," he said in the same sort of tone. "I normally had to keep watch over her, to make sure she was still breathing. More than once, I was convinced she wouldn't wake up. Joy to the world, indeed."

"I'm sorry," Hannah said at once. "I didn't mean—"

"I understand the utility of a Christmas program, whether in a restaurant or, indeed, in a hotel that is attempting to become a premiere location in a country filled with such places." He sounded almost impatient, now. "I also understand that this is some kind of test for you. You are expected to face it and in so doing, prove your worth."

Hannah cleared her throat. "That would, obviously, be the preferred outcome, to my way of thinking."

"I will tell you now that I find it unlikely that there will be any other outcome," Antonluca told her. Gruffly.

"Once Christmas is done, I will leave the hotel to you. There is very little that your capable hands cannot handle."

He looked so remote then, as cold as the blustery December day all around them, but something inside her seemed to twist in on itself. She had the strangest urge to reach out and put her hands on him. To make him feel better. To soothe him.

To do something about the ache she felt in her that she was certain came directly from him—

Thankfully, she controlled herself.

"That sounds as if we won't see you on the hotel floor," she said, and it cost her to sound so mild, yet upbeat. It actually *hurt*.

"You won't," he replied.

Hannah could tell that he'd...come to some decision then. It was the way he looked at her. It was that frozen sort of feeling, there between them.

It was the finality in the way he'd said that. *You won't*.

"I thought you lived on the next hill over. Or that's what I heard in the village, anyway."

"I have a great many houses," he told her, and it seemed...

She was sure that there was more happening here, in the thickening air between them, than it sounded like there was. Because she could feel it.

And this time it was more than a flutter.

"Of course you do," she agreed. "I believe that's the

whole point of being a celebrity billionaire chef, isn't it? The real estate alone."

"I'm happy to own a hotel, Hannah," he said in that brittle voice of his. "But that does not mean that I wish to run one." He lifted a brow. "If I did, I would have no need of you."

She told herself he could not possibly have meant to hurt her. He had simply stated a fact. Her feelings were her own problem.

But that didn't seem to ease the sting any.

"All I ask is that you keep your opinions to yourself, please," he said quietly.

Quietly, but there was all that intense gray behind it.

And somehow, out here where half of Tuscany was watching, they'd ended up standing far too close together. She felt her toes curl up in her boots. She felt herself flush all over, and was glad that today she'd thought to bundle up sufficiently that no one needed to know that but her.

"What I can promise," she said, "is that I'll keep my opinions out of the papers."

If it killed her.

"I thank you," he replied.

And she could hear that sardonic inflection. But she was looking up at him, and there was something so stark about his expression. Something that on anyone else, she might have called *lost*, there in the eyes.

She had never wanted to touch anyone as much as she wanted to touch him then.

But she didn't. She couldn't.

Instead, inside of her, she felt a great wave of shame—so intense that it hurt—because she still hadn't told him about Dominic.

This was the moment. This was well past the moment, in fact, and she had no excuse for that. There was no justification for it, not when she'd spent the past couple of weeks in his company, enough to know that he was no monster. He was not abusive, or vindictive.

On the contrary, she found that all this time talking to him and working with him didn't make her like him any less. Quite the opposite.

Tell him, she ordered herself. *Tell him now.*

But she couldn't bring herself to do it.

He was too close. His stormy gaze dropped from hers, down to her lips, and some kind of resolve took her over.

He was her boss. They had already kissed once, that first day in the library, but she thought that had been left over from before—from that night in New York. There was no need to go back there.

Because he'd said as much, hadn't he? He wasn't the sort to stay in one place. He had houses all over the world, like every other wealthy person she'd ever heard of. And when it came down to it, Hannah didn't need anything from him. She doubted very much that he would be at all interested in the child he'd made, and besides, if he said anything cruel about Dominic or made any move to harm her son, she would hate him forever.

It wasn't worth the risk.

Her son had her, and he had Cinzia. Dominic didn't need grandparents and other relatives who didn't care about him.

Maybe he also didn't need a father who didn't know he existed and was unlikely to care all that much if he did.

More to the point, he wouldn't even be around after Christmas. He'd said so himself. So what was the point of telling him now?

You are rationalizing, something in her hissed, but she shoved it aside.

"You do not look filled with the Christmas spirit at all," Antonluca said. "You look something more like murderous."

"I'm only in the Christmas spirit on Christmas itself," she replied, though as she said it she could hear that she sounded much sharper than she should. She tried to modify her tone. "And in the meantime, I really will murder someone if they don't set these tables up correctly."

She told herself that she merely stepped away to look after the details of the Christmas Market—to *do her job*, she assured herself—but she couldn't shake the notion that what she was really doing was running.

Like a coward.

But she told herself she was doing it for Dominic, and that made it okay.

She had to believe that made it okay.

CHAPTER FOUR

ANTONLUCA HAD ALWAYS hated Christmas. Whether it was memories of his unfortunate childhood or too many stressful kitchen environments during the holidays, who could say? The result was the same. He wasn't a fan.

Yet every day he spent at La Paloma, the more contagious its Christmas spirit seemed to be.

He couldn't say he liked that, either.

Especially when there seemed to be such a distinct link between the festive Christmas atmosphere in the hotel and the person responsible for making it that way.

One night, he found himself humming one of the Christmas carols that had been playing all day in the lobby and the rest of the common areas. One moment he had been celebrating another long day of keeping his hands to himself with a Negroni before a late meal in his otherwise deserted *castello*. The next he found himself entirely too close to singing about herald angels. He told himself he was revolted that he should have been infected by such an earworm—

But if there was any such contagion, it was Hannah.

Antonluca had stopped pretending some while ago

that he was looking for reasons to fire her again. There hadn't been a particular moment that had tipped him in that direction, or not one he recalled. He simply...hadn't considered terminating her. In ages.

He told himself this was simply good business. The truth was, she was excellent at what she did, as he had now seen firsthand. He had examined every possible detail of the hotel. He had monitored her for weeks now. There were no complaints to be made about her performance, because it was flawless.

She was flawless.

In fact, the only complaint Antonluca could really think of when it came to Hannah was that he hadn't seen her naked again.

He could have complained about that at great length. And rather thought it spoke to his virtue that he did not.

Despite any lingering earworms to disturb his *aperitivo*.

"Are you listening?" she asked after one meeting, sitting there once again in the confines of her ruthlessly impersonal office, during which he had entertained himself with a particularly detailed memory of the night in New York.

"I am nothing if not the very picture of attentiveness," he assured her.

Her green eyes lit with amusement. "Really. And yet, somehow, you have nothing to say about the kitchen's notes on your suggestions."

And Antonluca could not possibly admit, now, that he

hadn't been listening to what she'd been saying. Perish the thought. He shrugged instead. "I never have anything to say to notes," he told her with only slightly exaggerated arrogance. "I dismiss them immediately, with prejudice, and carry on as before."

"I see." But she looked as if she was trying not to laugh.

"If I were to comment on notes," Antonluca continued, because he was suddenly seized with the need to actually see her laugh. Just once. Surely that would... scratch this itch he didn't understand inside of him. "If I were to lower myself in such a fashion, I might point out that I did not make suggestions to the kitchen. I changed the menu. Input was not sought and will not be received."

He saw a flash of her smile at that and it felt like a sharp, wild joy, the same way he'd felt—so long ago now—when he'd tasted something he'd made once he'd gotten it right. That brightness like a song within him, and not one involving angels, herald or otherwise.

"I will pass that on," Hannah murmured in her appropriate, professional voice, though her eyes were gleaming.

And later, when he walked her out to her car as she left for the day—and did not question himself as to why he was dancing attendance on an employee—Antonluca found himself standing there on the old forecourt for some time after she drove away.

He had taken it upon himself to walk to and from the

hotel every day now, as the land was all his. And for other reasons, most of them involving getting his head on right and doing the closest thing to a cold shower without actually committing to one of those dreadful cold plunges. And besides, a brisk tramp in the December cold was an excellent way to remind himself that while his trappings might be soft these days, *he* was not.

Tonight, as he walked down into the fields and then wound his way through vineyards nestled down for the winter, it occurred to him that he had never spent this much time with a woman he wasn't related to without having sex.

It shocked him enough that he stopped walking for a moment, his breath making clouds against the dark.

Behind him, the hotel lolled about over one hillside, brightly shining into the night. On another hill ahead of him stood his castle, with only the one beacon of light high up on the old stone walls. And here he was caught in the valley between the two, the intensity of the winter darkness and that woman making him feel like a stranger to himself.

Again.

Antonluca had always enjoyed women, in the same way that he enjoyed other people's food. He liked the taste, the experience. But he was always hungry again—and rarely for the same thing.

What he had never done was get to know a woman like this.

All this talking. All this sitting around together,

studying things as one. All these conversations while they observed the way the hotel ran and exchanged their thoughts on it. If he recalled correctly, they hadn't spoken much at all that night in New York.

There had been far too many other things to do.

Here, now, the night was wet and cold, and he welcomed it. It pressed against him as he moved, a bit like it was fighting back, and he welcomed that, too. The cold seemed to seep into his bones, despite the very warm coat he wore, and whether he welcomed that or not, it was familiar.

It reminded him very much of the way Hannah seemed to have crept inside of him. As if she'd taken up residence in his bones herself, and that hadn't started when she'd walked into the hotel library.

He had thought about that night in New York…often.

Now, however, it was worse. The memories of that night haunted him. They kept him up at night. He would lie in his bed, staring at the ceiling, remembering every moment, every shift of their bodies, every breath and sigh.

Sometimes the ache was so intense that he would take his cock in his own hands and handle it himself.

And then, every morning, there she was again.

Bright. Gleaming. Seemingly completely unaffected by him in every way, and he couldn't understand why that made him want her more.

There was something about that sleek, cool exterior of hers that made him long to get his hands on her. To pull down that hair that she always kept in that subdued twist. To penetrate the armor of her elegant clothes, her carefully applied cosmetics—always a quiet enhancement, never a conversation piece.

He longed, with every part of him, to mess her up again.

Maybe it was because she had come to him that night in New York so emotional, so wide-open to whatever the night might bring.

To whatever happened between them, again and again and again.

This version of Hannah was far more circumspect.

It made him want to crack her open and find his way inside, any way he could.

He did not allow himself the pleasure. He vowed to himself that he would not. Mixing business and pleasure had never worked. Not for him when he was younger and tempestuous and far more foolish. And not for him with the woman he'd flown across the world to fire personally, either.

A wise man—like the one he aspired to be—would know better.

As the year wound down, his siblings began calling. They did not have the same feelings about the holidays as he did. But then, why would they? He was the reason their holidays had not been dire.

"When was the last time you came to Melbourne?" asked one of his sisters. "You're well overdue a bit of a summer Crimbo, don't you think?"

"Thank you for thinking of me," he replied dryly. "But I believe I would rather swim to Australia and be eaten by sharks en route then engage in anything called *Crimbo*."

His other siblings made similar demands. He ought to come to Los Angeles. He was welcome anytime in France and Germany.

It was perhaps unsurprising that his youngest sibling, Rocco, called for entirely different reasons. Rocco had been born when Antonluca was ten. By the time he was aware of the world, Antonluca was already successful. Rocco therefore hadn't struggled like the rest of them. Or not as much, anyway.

"What is this about a hotel?" Rocco demanded from Rome, where he was tasked with managing the original restaurant. Emiliano's. "Since when are we in the hotel business?"

"Are *we* in a business?" Antonluca asked, swirling his nightly Negroni in its tumbler as he glowered out his window at the hotel on the next hill. "You understand my confusion. I was under the impression that *I* ran a business and merely carry you all along with me, like so much ballast."

Some of his other siblings would have taken offense at that. Or worse, been hurt. Rocco only laughed.

"I've been saying that we should expand into hotels for years," he said stoutly, though Antonluca could not recall any instance of that occurring. Not in his hearing. "It just makes sense."

It was another late night. Antonluca had taken his time walking home, because Hannah had been working one of the hotel's events and had therefore been wearing an evening gown in place of her more typical daytime attire.

Now he did not need to remember the curve of her shoulder, the slope of her collarbone. Not from New York. Now he'd seen them again.

And yet had not been able to press his mouth to the pulse in her neck, or smooth his hands down the length of her body to cup her bottom, pull her close, and make them both groan—

The good thing about a call from Rocco was that it was distracting.

"I have never heard you mention a hotel or any expansion ideas of any kind," he told the youngest Aniello. "That must be the sort of thing you tell those idiots you carouse with all over Europe, funded entirely by my legacy."

That set him to thinking about legacies. This castle, for example. He had thought it a daring, over-the-top purchase back in the day, but he'd never regretted it. This was the place he came to when he wanted to hear himself think. This was the place that was entirely his and did not exist only because he provided services to those who came here.

No one asked him for anything here. He kept a skeleton staff because after a lifetime of too many siblings and restaurants filled with various dependents, he needed very little but his own company.

It was here that he'd spent a lot of time in the kitchens, wishing he felt inspired to experiment again.

It was here that he'd come to the conclusion that his experimentation days were over and what he had before him instead was the bolstering of his reputation, and that legacy he intended to outlive him and all the rest of his siblings, Rocco included.

"Your legacy is a generous benefactor," his brother was saying. "*Grazie.* As for your new hobby, why don't I come and manage it? Just think what I could do with a hotel."

"If you want a hotel, I'm sure we can find you one." Antonluca had showered off the cold and now stood at the window with his *aperitivo*, the way he did every night. He stared across the expanse of fields and vineyards drenched in the dark to that hill in the distance, where the hotel gleamed against the night.

Like his very own star of Bethlehem.

"What's wrong with the one you have now?" Rocco asked. Perhaps with a slight hint of belligerence in his otherwise easygoing tone.

"La Paloma already has a manager," Antonluca told him. "And quite a talented one."

"She might be talented," his brother argued, which told Antonluca that Rocco had been paying much closer attention to what happened in Tuscany than he'd imagined. "But she's not family, is she?"

And that stung a little because Antonluca had always been open about the fact he liked to keep things in the family. It was easier that way. Not that his siblings couldn't squabble amongst themselves, because they did. But each and every one of them felt a deep connection to one another because they'd all made it out of their childhoods. They'd survived.

They felt even more connected to Antonluca because he was the reason why.

No need to worry about motivations when it was family.

What he found was that he really didn't like being reminded of this.

"She is not," Antonluca agreed, a bit more icily than necessary. "But I trust her just the same."

And it wasn't until a couple of days later that he realized he could not have said anything that could have alarmed his brother more.

He realized this because when he finished walking home that night, the week before Christmas, he found Rocco waiting for him in the grand hall of his castle. With some stranger beside him, looking snobbish and pinched-faced.

Antonluca took against the stranger immediately.

"To what do I owe this entirely unexpected and unsolicited honor?" he asked his brother. "And who is watching over the restaurant in Rome if you're here?"

"I also have a manager." Rocco waved a hand. "You

have to listen to what this man is here to tell you, *fratello*. It's important."

Antonluca doubted that very much, but he ushered the men into one of his sitting rooms, called for his single member of staff, and took his time showering and changing his clothes before he went down to join them.

Rocco was lounging in Antonluca's favorite chair when he returned—and knew it, judging from the smirk on his face—but the stranger was standing by the fireplace, looking stiff and ill at ease.

"Forgive me," Antonluca said, barely sparing the stranger a glance. "I find anticipation makes me hungry. Perhaps a meal while we—"

"I will get this out and then take my leave," the stranger belted out.

Rocco's eyes widened. Antonluca merely stared at him.

He was not used to being interrupted. Particularly not by uninvited strangers in his home.

"My apologies," he replied after some long moments, with scathing courtesy. "I have clearly forgotten myself. Of course I want any guests in my home, invited or not, to feel at ease when they arrive without warning."

But his sardonic words were lost on the stranger. The pinched-faced man puffed himself up, standing taller and looking even more pompous. "I used to be the manager at La Paloma," he intoned, and managed to give off the impression that he was offended Antonluca did not already know this, and recognize him. "I was tossed out without so much as a thank-you by that evil old witch and replaced with—"

"The current manager, yes," Antonluca interrupted him smoothly, before this man called Hannah a name. It was bad enough that he had spoken so disrespectfully about Paloma. He already disliked the man.

But if he said the same kind of things about Hannah, Antonluca rather thought that he might end him.

"Your current manager is a woman of low morals," the man told Antonluca.

Meaning, of course, that Antonluca began plotting his death immediately. Perhaps he could simply toss the man off the battlements, the way the ancients who'd built this place had surely done with their enemies. Otherwise, there would be no need for battlements, would there?

"Raffaele still has family in the village," Rocco chimed in then, perhaps reading the look on his older brother's face. "There's nothing that happens around here that he doesn't know about."

"Is that so?" But that was less a question and more a threat, the way Antonluca said it.

"She turned up about two and a half years ago," Raffaele said with great, whining umbrage, which did not endear him to his host in any way. "Like most Americans, she made no attempt whatsoever to integrate herself into the village. Instead, she thought that she could simply appear and everything would be handed to her. Just as my own job was."

He lapsed off into a tirade that was mostly a list of

complaints about Paloma, and Antonluca shifted his gaze to his brother. Rocco knew exactly how Antonluca felt about complaining. That he always wanted solutions, not feelings.

But Rocco made a face at him, as if there was something in all of these complaints that should matter to him.

"I'm sorry that you feel that you were cruelly treated," Antonluca said shortly when Raffaele finally paused for breath. "But I'm afraid I can't help you with any of that. Paloma is no longer involved in the hotel. And I did not fire you."

"Your brother wanted to know about this manager of yours," Raffaele said, sounding somehow even more aggrieved. "And I say again, she is a woman of *extremely* low morals. I would not be surprised if she keeps some kind of a *side business* going out of the cottage she rents."

Antonluca decided that the man could not possibly mean what it sounded like he meant.

"You perhaps mean some crafting?" he asked, dangerously. "The sort of thing that can be sold in the Christmas Market, I imagine?"

His brother had the sense to look alarmed, and rose from the chair he'd been lounging in. But the stranger Antonluca had decided he disliked intensely enough to perhaps relive the more violent days of his misspent youth let out a bitter sort of laugh.

"She moved here pregnant," he said with a sniff of

disgust. "And all alone. And there has never been a man in the picture. She is simply a sad single mother who ran off from her own country to hide her shame in Tuscany. Aren't you tired of these people? I know I am."

He launched off into another tirade, but Antonluca stopped listening.

Because all he could think about was timing.

Two and a half years ago.

Already pregnant.

What were the chances…?

But he knew that chance had nothing to do with this.

He didn't need to hear another word from this weasel of a man. He needed to hear it from Hannah directly. He needed to *know*.

Because down deep in his bones, as if his DNA recognized what it was being told without a single shred of proof—he was already sure.

Hannah had a child.

And if Hannah had a child after the night she had given her innocence to him in New York, well.

He was absolutely certain, sight unseen, that it was his.

CHAPTER FIVE

HANNAH MADE IT home later that evening. The event had gone off without a hitch, and she was pleased about that, but she was even more pleased that she managed to get home in time to snuggle Dominic on his way to bed.

And then sit and have dinner with her neighbor and friend, as she got to do too seldomly.

"You never seem tired when you come home," the older woman noted as they shared wine and broke bread together. "I think this job suits you."

What Hannah thought was that her current companion at the job suited her, but she refused to say that out loud. It was tempting fate, surely.

More than that, it was entirely predicated on a lie of omission. If she was wise, she would stop pretending to herself that there was any way out of the situation she was in that wouldn't leave someone hurt. Likely herself.

Just as long as it's not Dominic, she thought fiercely.

But then, wasn't she the one making sure that he *would* be hurt? By drawing out the inevitable moment of truth with the one man who could hurt them all?

After Cinzia left, Hannah went in to check on Dominic—or, if she was honest with herself, to try to make herself feel better about the choices she was making. And the quicksand it seemed she was standing in.

"I need to tell him," she whispered as she stood there, staring down at her perfect little boy in his crib. It was hard to imagine that soon—any moment now, really, and it was possible she was dragging her feet on this— it was going to be time for a bigger bed. It seemed like only a blink since he was red and wrinkled and new, and spent most of his time a hot weight against her body. And everyone said the time only went faster and faster.

Would she blink again and find her tiny baby boy a whole grown man?

Yet even thinking that made the guilt inside of her seem to swell and ripen, until she was terribly afraid something would burst. She knew she needed to tell Antonluca. She knew it, and every night she resolved that tomorrow would be the day—

But it never was, was it?

It turned out that Hannah really wasn't the woman she'd always believed herself to be. The woman she'd been so sure she was, without question. She had been indiscreet with her friend in New York, yes, but *she* wasn't the betraying kind *herself*. That distinction had always seemed critical to her.

And wasn't it a bitter pill to swallow that she was, maybe, more like that terrible friend of hers than not?

In the crib he could already climb out of, Dominic shifted slightly. Hannah gazed down at his sooty dark lashes as they rested there against his round, plump cheeks. The urge to wake him up just so she could kiss him on those cheeks and love on him some more was almost overwhelming, but she was used to that. She suspected that it would never get any better or any easier to keep from adoring this child.

She suspected this was simply motherhood.

Why shouldn't Antonluca get to feel the same way? she asked herself as she crept out of the room, her heart full.

And also aching a little bit, she acknowledged as she went back to the main room. But she didn't know what to do about that aside from the obvious, first chance she got, so she busied herself tidying things up, though it wasn't exactly necessary. Cinzia was always good about leaving things a bit cleaner than she found them.

Another way her neighbor was perfect, to Hannah's mind.

She was contemplating whether to settle in on the cozy sofa with a book and a glass of wine, or whether she might take both of those things into the bath with her for a soak, when there was a sudden, loud, *demanding* sort of thumping sound.

It took her a long moment to understand that it was the door.

That there was someone *at* her door, which made no sense.

She stood where she was and stared at it, confused when the thumping started again. Until she realized that there had to be someone *standing there*, pounding on the door with a fist.

But whether or not she found this personally alarming, what made her furious was thinking that someone thought they could come and make that much noise when there was a baby sleeping.

Not on Hannah's watch.

She hurtled herself toward the door and flung it open, prepared to give whoever was standing there a piece of her mind—

But it was Antonluca.

And he looked… More intense than she'd ever seen him before. Almost *vibrating* with that intensity and, if she wasn't mistaken, somewhat…ragged around the edges, besides. Or maybe it was simply that he was in casual clothes, when she'd never seen him in anything but a suit. Suggesting he'd come rushing here from his home.

"What…?" she began, her mind already wondering what calamity could have befallen the hotel in the few short hours since she'd left for the night. Already thinking that she could go back inside and grab a coat to throw over the sweater and lounging pants she was wearing, both quite a few notches above regular sweats, if not exactly up to her typical standards for the office—

"Is it true?" Antonluca gritted out.

It was cold out there tonight. She could hear the wind causing a ruckus. It smelled like snow. The dark seemed to press in on her. "I have no idea what you're—"

"Is it true, Hannah?" he asked again, his voice darker. Rougher. "Do you have a child?"

And Hannah felt herself go terribly, frighteningly still. As if the world stopped turning, with a sudden, scary jolt.

She was a bit surprised that she wasn't tossed straight off.

Or maybe she wished she was, because she couldn't speak. She had never seen his gray eyes so dark, so haunted. She had never seen that mobile face of his, always so beautifully masculine, look so twisted. So anguished.

She had to say something. She *needed* to say anything.

But Hannah couldn't seem to make her throat move or her mouth form words. Still seized up and frozen solid, she managed to nod her head.

Just the faintest little bit.

Yet it was enough.

Antonluca was filling up her doorway and then he leaned in, and it seemed to her that he put his face dangerously close to hers as the world began spinning again, too fast.

"Did you…? *Do you* have my child?" he asked, though it was more the suggestion of words. She wasn't sure his voice made any real sound at all.

Hannah felt her eyes prick with emotion. She felt her chest go tight and full.

But she could have done this already and she hadn't.

This was on her. She cleared her throat. She nodded again, more jerkily this time, to make sure he saw it. To make sure she was really doing it. "I found out I was pregnant after I moved home to Nebraska. I had no way to contact you. I didn't even know your name."

"But you know it now," he pointed out in that low, dangerous voice. "You have known it for some while, have you not."

It wasn't a question.

He moved then and she stepped back immediately.

And only realized after he swept into her cottage and she closed the door behind him by rote, to keep the cold out, that she really should have thought this through.

Because all of that seething fury on her doorstep was one thing, but it was something else *inside* the cottage itself. Moments ago she'd been thinking how cozy it was here, how bright and happy even in the darkest part of the year.

Now it was as if the darkness had taken over.

He was a shock against all that brightness, the brutal masculine beauty of him so tall and lean and furious right here in the middle of all this feminine space.

Antonluca made no attempt to look around, or make any small talk. He stood there in the middle of the room and stared at Hannah.

Through her, more like.

She swallowed hard, and didn't bother trying to offer any kind of explanation. Instead, she moved across the room and beckoned him to follow her, though she lifted a finger to her lips as she eased open Dominic's door.

Inside, the little boy was still fast asleep in his crib.

Beside her, Antonluca made a small sound, almost beneath his breath. But she heard it.

It made her heart kick at her, so hard it made her ribs ache.

And there was something exquisitely painful—though whether it was a terrible joy or a kind of loss, she couldn't have said—to watch as the man that she'd created this perfect little boy with beheld him for the first time.

There was something almost sacred about it. Hannah found her hands over her mouth as Antonluca moved to the edge of the crib and looked down, that dark fury on his face changing almost at once to something that could only be wonder.

He put his hand out and she almost stopped him, but she thought better of it.

And so she watched as gently—so very gently that she thought she might start sobbing—he settled that big hand of his on Dominic's belly.

For a long, beautiful, impossible moment, it was as if they all breathed together.

Hannah watched as Dominic's faint restlessness went away. As if he knew his father's hand and the heat that came from it.

As if he'd been waiting for exactly this to truly settle him down.

And still, it was the look on Antonluca's face that almost undid her. There was something so bright and sharp in his gaze. There was something about the way he held his mouth, a tenderness she hadn't imagined a man so gorgeous could possess. She wasn't close enough to him to hear what he whispered over the sleeping figure of the little boy, like some kind of prayer.

Her heart thought it knew.

But then it didn't matter, because when he straightened from the crib and turned back to her, his face was like thunder.

Hannah could hardly bear to look at him, though she was equally incapable of looking away. But she had to give him her back as she led him out of the room again, and it wasn't any better when she faced him again on the other side of Dominic's bedroom wall, his door shut once more.

And then they were standing there, facing each other, in the main room of this little cottage that had never felt smaller. That, in fact, seemed to shrink more with every breath.

Once again, Hannah cast around for the right words to say to make this... Well. Not *better*. But understandable, anyway. Because it had made a kind of sense to her...

Yet nothing came to her, because there wasn't anything to say.

There wasn't any making this understandable.

And with every breath, every second that she continued to not speak, she could feel it all get darker and stormier and more furious between them.

She couldn't blame him, but she still couldn't manage to get a single word out.

"What I want to know—" and Antonluca's voice was so low and so furious that it seemed to shiver through her "—is if all of this was deliberate."

Hannah started to speak then, but had to clear her throat. "I don't know what that means."

"Why did you come to Italy?" he demanded. "But why start there? We can go back even further. Did you plant that story in the newspapers because you knew how I would react? Has this all been a setup from the start?"

She blinked at that, that feeling of paralysis leaving her, slowly. But surely. "A setup?" She asked that carefully, as if she needed to sound out the words. "You think someone would set up…a whole baby?"

"I think many women would do exactly that, and happily."

"I didn't know who you were. If I had known, I would have told you the moment I discovered I was pregnant." She kept her voice even, or as close to even as she could, under the circumstances. "Instead, I shamed my entire family, was unwelcome in my childhood home, and decided to go make a life for myself and my child elsewhere. Why would I have done any of that if, all along, I could have reached out to you instead?"

"You truly want me to believe that you just happened

upon this village, out of all the villages in Italy?" She had never seen him like this, and all she could think was that he was so *big*. He towered over her. And there was that anguish and that fury all over him, making it so she couldn't decide if she wanted to reach out to him. Or run. "You *just happened* to find your way here from Nebraska, of all places?"

"I have always wanted to go to Italy," she told him in a low voice, aware that her hands were in fists at her sides. "It had nothing to do with you."

He leaned closer. "Bullshit."

She felt as if he'd slapped her, but she made herself stand straighter. "I can't defend my choices. I should have told you the moment I walked into that library. I honestly don't know why I didn't."

He made a low, furious sound. "Neither do I."

Hannah pushed on. "But before that, none of the choices I made had anything to do with you. I wasn't trying to get close to you. I couldn't have even if I'd wanted to because I didn't know who you were." She made sure to emphasize that as she said it. Again. His storm cloud eyes flashed, so she continued. "We did very little talking that night, as you may recall. And in the morning, I was called into the restaurant to stand and accept two hours of yelling, and I did. I took all of that as my due. *You* weren't there. I had no idea I'd ever met Antonluca, world-famous chef. I simply got fired, licked my wounds a bit, and then sorted myself out as best I could. All by myself because I had no way to even contact you, whether I knew who you were or not."

He made another low, furious sort of sound but he didn't say anything. This time.

Hannah made herself pull in a breath, though she couldn't seem to unclench her fists. "By the time I realized I was pregnant, I'd been in Nebraska for a month and a half. Maybe more. I thought about attempting to call the restaurant to find out who that man had been at the bar that night. But how would I do that? Who do you think would speak to me at that point?"

And she saw him actually take that on board. He knew how tight-knit and sometimes toxic restaurants were. He knew how everyone banded together—as much for self-preservation as loyalty.

There was no way anyone who wanted to keep working at that restaurant would risk being the one to tell someone like Hannah—who had drawn fire from above and was persona non grata in restaurant circles—something that might end up getting them in hot water, too. It wasn't worth the risk.

He had to know that. She could see that he did.

Hannah watched as he accepted that, though he clearly didn't like it.

"Fine," he said, his voice darker than she'd ever heard it. "I can understand that. But there is no justification for you not telling me here. The very moment you recognized me in that very first meeting."

"I agree." But he was staring at her as if he wanted

her to justify it all the same. "You won't understand. And I don't blame you, either. All I can do is tell you that I wasn't trying to hurt you. I was trying to protect Dominic."

"Dominic." He said the name and he said it again, with more of Italian flair, beneath his breath. And she felt it like music inside of her. "You named the baby Dominic?"

"Yes," she said. "His name is Dominic." And she was aware that something in her was shaking. Trembling. "I... I've always liked that name."

She watched as he took that in. As he raised his hands to his face as if he needed to rub understanding into his own skin.

Then something in her hitched a bit when she saw that he was shaking, too.

"I knew that once I told you everything would change," Hannah made herself say, and it sounded so silly when she said it out loud. So selfish and small in the face of the simple truth that she had *concealed his own child* from him. What had she been thinking? "And I didn't want things to change. I like this life exactly as it is."

He made a sound, and she hurried on. "I'm not defending myself. Really, I'm not. I'm just telling you how and why—"

"My back story is sanitized," he told her, and that dark gray gaze of his seemed to pin her to the wall even though they were standing away from it. "Everyone loves the story of a scrappy rise from modest beginnings, but no one wants to know what it was really like. Do you, Hannah?"

She had the distinct feeling that, in fact, she did not want to know. "What I want to say most of all," she tried to say in a rush, "is that I'm so very sorry—"

"Oh, no," he said, cutting her off, his voice deceptively gentle when the look in his eyes was anything but. And made her blood seem to chill and then light itself up at once. "No apologies, Hannah. It is too late for that."

"But..."

Antonluca slashed a hand through the air, and she fell silent.

"My mother was a prostitute," he told her flatly. Matter-of-factly, she would have said, if she hadn't been able to see the look in his eyes. "If you ask my siblings, they will tell you that she had trouble with drugs. That is also true, but that's not the whole story. Her pregnancies were all deliberate, as she thought that would curry favor with the men who controlled what she did. It never worked."

Hannah stared at him, feeling paralyzed once again. Because she knew his story the same as anyone else did. A stunning rise from poverty thanks to a benevolent restaurant owner, a bit of dishwashing to make it relatable before the Michelin stars and widespread acclaim, and the rest was history. She supposed that when she thought about it, she'd assumed that the poverty he'd risen from was more...genteel.

A bit more entertaining than upsetting, if she'd had to guess. More cheeky orphan makes good than desperate climb from a swamp.

And she was sure that no one had ever mentioned *prostitution* when they'd been spinning these tales of the self-made, self-taught chef who took the culinary world by surprise, then reigned over it as he pleased.

"I have three brothers and two sisters, all younger than me," Antonluca was telling her in the same fierce, flat way. "And it was clear to me exactly what future we all had in store for us if I didn't do something. So I did it."

"That only makes what you've made of your life more extraordinary," she said quietly. "I hope you know that."

But if anything, that seemed to incense him further.

"What I know is that I vowed back then that I would never bring another child into this world," he bit out at her in that same low, furious voice. "I have already raised five."

And Hannah felt guilty. She could have handled all of this better, clearly. Maybe she should have tried harder to find him while she was still pregnant. But even if that really had been as impossible as she'd found it at the time, what she really and truly could not account for was why she hadn't told him over the past couple of weeks.

Maybe she would feel guilty about that forever. Maybe that was a price she would have to pay.

But that didn't mean she'd forgotten some of the key details of the night in question.

"If that was the case," she said now, tipping her chin up, "then perhaps you should have paid more attention to birth control while having acrobatic sex with a stranger."

And then, for the first time in as long as she'd known him—which seemed a good deal longer than it actually had been—Antonluca laughed.

It was not a nice laugh.

It seemed to cascade over her, a rush of heat. It kicked up brush fires and deeper shivers, and any number of other reactions she really could have done without.

"Do you really dare?" he demanded, his voice so dark it seemed to bring the cold in again. "Do you *dare* to say such a thing to me after what you have done?"

"I'm just suggesting that while we're taking responsibility for our actions here tonight, perhaps you could join in," Hannah retorted.

She was aware that this was not the most prudent course of action. She was fully cognizant of the fact that this, right here, could be the end of everything she'd worked for. Worse than that, this would almost certainly have implications for Dominic.

But she couldn't seem to stop herself.

Not when he was bearing down on her like he held the flaming sword of righteousness in one hand.

"Were you a virgin?" she asked him.

Another hard, brittle laugh. "Hardly."

"I was." She couldn't imagine how he could have forgotten that. Either way, she threw it at him like a weapon. "I told you so. And yet I ended up pregnant. Who do you think was to blame for that?"

"I know who I blame for it," he seethed back at her. "That would be the woman who has somehow wormed her way into every part of my life. Do you think that this will go unchallenged? Do you think that I will simply…succumb to this?"

"To parenthood?" she threw back at him. "No worries on that account, Antonluca. *You* don't have to do anything. I've been taking care of Dominic since the day he was born. Since before that, in fact. I've done it all on my own. Your name isn't on his birth certificate, because I didn't know it. You have no responsibility here at all. If you like, you can turn around and walk back out that door and we can both pretend that this moment of reckoning never happened." She shrugged, a bit theatrically, but it was all she had. She lifted her chin higher. "That's fine with me."

"Unfortunately for you, *diavolessa*," he growled at her, "it is not at all fine with me."

And it was only then she realized that they were in the danger zone. That they were much too close. That he had somehow backed her against the wall and she'd been too busy trying to fight him to notice.

But she certainly noticed now.

Because he muttered something in Italian that she didn't quite catch, though she could feel the words all over her, and then he slammed his mouth to hers.

And it was as if they simply *ignited*.

It was a bolt of lightning, and then they tore into each other.

This was nothing like that night in New York.

This was a fury.

This was hurt and temper, all wrapped up in the way his mouth moved on hers and the way his hands gripped her hair.

It was a terrible, exhilarating fury.

Hannah tore at his shirt and he tore at hers, and then, somehow, she was in his arms. Then her legs were wrapped tight around his waist, and he was working one of his hands between them as he slammed her back into the wall.

Then, with a thrust that she could feel from her toes to the tips of her ears, he slammed himself fully inside of her.

And the wildest part of all was that she was ready for him.

She was more than ready, though he was even bigger than she remembered.

And he filled her completely, sinking so deep that she was shaking immediately.

Then she was falling apart, his name in her mouth as he pounded her straight through one wild orgasm into another.

Then another still.

And only then was he was coming, too, following her lead, muttering what sounded like curses against her neck.

Then there was nothing but the loud panting of their breath.

An aftermath that hurt almost as much as all that had...not hurt. At all.

His dark eyes glittered as he pulled himself free, setting her feet back down on the floor. He stepped away, pulling his clothing to rights, and she didn't like how disheveled he looked. How wild-eyed he was.

Because she imagined she was worse.

"Antonluca—" she began.

"*Basta*," he said harshly. "You are finished making decisions where my son is concerned, Hannah. This is all finished."

She didn't know what he meant by that.

Or rather, she could speculate, though she didn't want to.

"I don't know what that means," she said quietly. While her entire body thrummed with leftover passion, and rather too much shame and guilt besides. "But I am his mother. There will be no decisions made about his life that do not involve me."

"Sleep on that," Antonluca suggested, as he shrugged back into a coat she hadn't seen him take off, hiding the shirt she'd ripped. "Tell yourself whatever you wish. But know this."

And he moved so fast then that she didn't see him coming.

One moment they were staring at each other, and the

next, his hands were on either side of her head and his face was in hers.

She heard herself gulp. Maybe it was more of a squeak.

"You betrayed me," he told her, while his gray eyes seemed to blaze deep inside of her, setting new fires. "You will not have the opportunity to do it again. And if you try, you won't like what happens. Maybe you should have a stint without your child to see how it feels, since you are so sanguine about such things."

And with that threat between them, he stared at her for another long moment, so long that she was sure she saw something almost give way—

But instead, he pushed himself away from the wall—from her—and then stormed back out into the night.

Leaving Hannah there against the wall with nothing to do but sink down to the floor, bury her head into her hands, and let all that emotion inside of her pour out as it would.

Quietly, though, so as not to wake the baby that Antonluca was welcome to love—but would be taking away from her only if he first climbed over her dead body to do it.

CHAPTER SIX

ANTONLUCA DIDN'T SLEEP, and not only because he wished he hadn't suggested he would take a small boy from his mother like he was auditioning to become any number of the terrible men who'd had too much influence over his own childhood.

Of course he wouldn't do such a thing.

He had built himself an entire life to make certain that not only could no one do such things to him, but that no one could do these things to his siblings, either. He had made certain they were all protected.

Obviously he could do no less for his own son.

Still, he stayed up all night and made certain that his legal team got as little sleep as he did. He barked out orders and demanded action as if that could take away the sting that seemed to get deeper—and become more of a low, long ache—the longer he sat with it.

And there was nothing to do *but* sit with it.

Hannah had betrayed him.

He kept circling back to that because he could have really sunk in deep on the betrayal aspect. But he didn't stay there—much as he might have wished he could, and even tried—because the real truth was that he had betrayed himself.

First that night in New York itself. He hadn't been nearly as militant about birth control as he had been for the whole of his life before then. A lot like the way he'd betrayed himself again this very same night, less than twenty minutes after he'd looked at the sleeping consequences of precisely that same behavior.

It was as if he'd wanted this all along.

But he knew that he had not.

He never had.

None of his siblings had partners or children, either. They were all proud of this, after the circumstances of their birth and early years. They had all watched their mother make a mess of every relationship she encountered, especially the one she'd had with them.

What they'd always had was each other. That and the empire that Antonluca had built. That was surely all the family anyone should need.

But now Antonluca had a son.

A son, he kept repeating to himself. *My son*.

The astonishingly perfect Dominic, who had looked nothing short of angelic lying there in that crib. There in that soft, sweet little cottage that was warm and bright and smelled like roses.

Nothing like anyplace Antonluca had ever lived as a child.

It made his chest hurt.

He paced around and around his castle, happy that

Rocco and that awful Raffaele were nowhere to be found. And at the first hint of morning light he found himself driving once again, following the winding roads into the village and then down to the base of the farthest hill, where a cluster of cottages were tucked into what must be a slope of glorious green come spring.

Even on a frigid, foggy December morning, it looked idyllic.

Antonluca had the strangest notion that his son was already living a life far better than the one he'd had when he was Dominic's age.

That made his chest hurt, too. If differently than before.

And this time, when he pounded on her door, Hannah opened it with a wariness in her gaze and the little boy on her hip.

The wide-awake little boy, now, with grave gray eyes that Antonluca recognized all too well. He saw them in his own mirror every day.

"Good morning." He thought Hannah sounded unreasonably calm and measured for a woman he'd had up against the wall in a sheer, blinding rush of temper—he told himself it had to have been temper, because he didn't like to think what else it could have been—only a few scant hours before.

He had the distinct and nearly ungovernable urge to do it again, but there was a child to consider.

Not just any child. This was *his* child. This was *his* son.

It took some getting used to.

And in the light of day, he could see that the little boy not only had his eyes, but was fixing those eyes directly on Antonluca. While sucking his two middle fingers in his mouth, the way almost all of Antonluca's siblings always had.

"Say *buongiorno*, Dominic," Hannah coached the toddler. She glanced at Antonluca—only a quick brush of her green eyes that he felt everywhere, in ways that suggested *temper* had nothing to do with this—and then she returned her gaze to the child. "Say '*Buongiorno, Papa*.'"

Antonluca felt everything in him go still. This wasn't what he wanted. Surely, this couldn't be real life, not when—

But the toddler lifted his dark head from his mother's shoulder, his gaze still disconcertingly direct. He removed those fingers from his mouth.

"*Buongiorno, Papa*," he said in a bright and happy little boy's voice.

And something deep inside of Antonluca seemed to… break in half. As if everything he had ever been or ever would be simply…

Changed.

In that simple, indelible moment, he was made new. Like it or not.

While he was trying his best to put himself back together, Hannah leveled another look at him—no less direct nor grave than their son's. Then she stepped back and allowed him inside once again.

He didn't know why he followed when everything in him was screaming at him to run. Maybe the trouble was that he didn't know whether he wanted to run *toward her* or *away from her.*

Maybe that had been the issue with Hannah Hansen from the very start.

He followed her into the cottage's one main room, and it was just as he remembered it from the night before. Even with toys strewn across the floor, it was bright and cozy.

Happy.

Nothing like the grimy flats—if they'd been lucky enough to have a flat, that was—that he recalled from his own childhood.

Hannah went to the brightly colored woven rug in the center of the floor and sat down, setting the little boy onto his feet beside her. He was happy to stand, and then peered up at the strange man in his house. Hannah, meanwhile, looked up as if she expected Antonluca to ponce about and avoid the toddler like the sticky gingered plague he likely was, but if there was one thing in this world that Antonluca knew better than he'd like to, it was children.

He found himself sitting down on the rug, too, then quickly getting drawn into an inspired discussion about the merits of plush toys versus little race cars with this tiny, chirpy human, who spoke in a mix of Italian and English and lisped his way through it all.

Antonluca became so engrossed in this debate that

he almost forgot where he was. Until he looked up and saw Hannah looking at him, her eyes shining.

The finest green he'd ever seen, he couldn't help but think.

"Stay where you are," she told him softly. "I'm going to make Dominic some breakfast."

He thought about the occasions his mother had cooked for them. There weren't many, and it had never been breakfast. That had been a *fend for yourself* affair, and God help you if you were the one who woke their mother while she slept. "What does Dominic eat?" he asked.

"Today, pancakes." Hannah blinked, then looked at him, her gaze guarded. "Would you like a pancake, too?"

Antonluca couldn't help but think how strange this was. How they were treating each other with such odd formality after what was not, by any definition, a *formal* interaction last night. And when they were both here, sitting on the floor with a small child and a collection of toys.

"Thank you," he said, though he had meant to say no. And then he heard himself continue, "I haven't had a regular pancake in years. That would be lovely."

He stayed where he was, sitting with Dominic as Hannah got to her feet, and moved across the airy main room into the open-plan kitchen area. Then he had to try to concentrate on every last detail of this miraculous little boy in front of him while also being keenly aware of the things Hannah was doing in her kitchen.

He heard the stove click on as she lit it. He smelled sweet butter warm in the pan, heard her stir with efficiency in a glass bowl, then listened to the sizzle of batter.

What he could not remember, however, was the last time that anyone had cooked for him. He was not certain that anyone ever had, unless, of course, he had deliberately gone to patronize their restaurant. But such occasions were rarely intimate.

Not like this.

And there was something about this—or perhaps he meant there was something about *her*—that seemed to fill him up from within this morning no matter how furious he ought to have been with her. Because Hannah seemed to have no qualms at all about serving a world-renowned chef with a selection of Michelin stars to his name a very simple pancake she'd whipped up in this rustic kitchen. From, if he was not mistaken, a premade boxed mix.

If she gave any of those things the faintest bit of thought, he saw no evidence of it as she set an old, chipped blue plate down beside him.

But he had to think that it was her very matter-of-factness, with no hint of anything even resembling preciousness, that was the reason *why* this pancake he ate sitting cross-legged on the floor with a child would rate higher than many desperately indulgent meals he'd eaten all over the world.

He couldn't decide if he was pleased or humbled by this.

Yet more fascinating by far, he told himself when he was finished quietly rhapsodizing about *pancakes*, was watching Dominic. He would have recognized the child even if he hadn't known who he was and where he'd come from, because he looked like all the rest of them. That dark hair. His gray eyes. That particular, mischievous smile—though Dominic smiled a good deal more easily than anyone in Antonluca's family ever had.

"He seems healthy and happy," he acknowledged later, the taste of sweet pancakes still on his tongue.

"He is both," Hannah replied. Her green gaze met his with a hint of affront. "Of course." She seemed to consider the implications, then frowned at him. "Did you have some doubt?"

"I have nothing but doubt," he told her, perhaps more darkly than he should have—but he could still taste the food she'd prepared for him, when no one dared prepare food for him, and the betrayal of this all seemed to hit him more keenly. "You tell me whether or not you would trust a person who kept your own child hidden from you."

"In future, you should perhaps give your one-night stands your name," Hannah replied crisply, though she smiled at the little boy when he looked at her. Then lost the smile when she looked back at Antonluca. "Just to get ahead of this trouble you find yourself in."

"I see that I'm not the only one who stayed up all night, coming up with clever replies to wield at will."

"I told you last night that I'm sorry that I didn't tell you about Dominic the moment I saw you here," Hannah said then. But her gaze stayed grave on his. "I meant that. But there's nothing I could have changed about what happened before that."

"This is what I do not understand," he said, almost as if he was musing aloud to himself. They were both speaking in quiet tones while the little boy sang songs to himself and played between them, though he doubted very much that either he or Hannah were fooled by the kind, polite tones. Not when they could see each other. "On the one hand, you're woman of great indiscretion, a liar and a betrayer. And yet, on the other hand, your work at the hotel speaks for itself. You have an unparalleled gift."

He expected her to throw something back at him, but all she did was glare.

"Can you explain this?" he asked.

Her gaze did not waver from his. "Can you explain the contradiction of having an aversion to both children and the preventative measures to avoid having them?"

"It is not a problem I have had with anyone but you," he heard himself growl at her. When he was certain he had not meant to say a thing.

When he was even more certain that he kept revealing himself here.

Hannah only shrugged. "Same."

And again, as usual, he felt that *pull* to her. It wasn't new. He had felt it that night in the restaurant in New York. He had felt it in the library when he'd thought his dreams were coming true in front of him.

If he was honest, he had felt it every moment since.

What intrigued him in this moment was that he watched her wary eyes change, shifting shades of green to the spark of emerald fire he saw now.

As if she was remembering last night the way he did.

Less a blast of temper and more…a reckoning. A remembering.

A reconnection every bit as cataclysmic as that first night in New York.

Because what they both knew now is that there was no pretending any longer. All truths were told and there was still all that wildfire between them, all that glory and need—

And he didn't know what might have happened then, but the front door of the cottage was thrown open without warning and an older woman Antonluca thought looked vaguely familiar—in the way all Italian women of a certain age did, though to be fair, all of the residents of the village here did, too—came bustling through.

"I am so sorry I am late," the old woman began cheerfully, "but I had to sing a whole song to the plants in my greenhouse and—" She stopped dead at the sight of Antonluca, there on the woven rug in the center of the floor. "What are you—?"

Hannah flushed. "Cinzia. I—"

But the old woman looked from Antonluca to the boy, then back again, her gaze a canny sort of thing. "Oh," she said, and she drew the syllable out and out and out. "I see. *Capisco*."

Antonluca found himself standing then, as if he had to prove himself to this woman. Or, more alarming, as if he wanted to make a good impression, a notion that was so absurd he nearly laughed at it then and there. "I am—"

"I can see who you are," the old woman replied, with far too much *understanding* in her voice. So much so that Hannah flushed yet again. "But in addition to more personal connections in this cottage, I think you are also the new owner of the hotel, are you not?"

What was there to say to that?

Antonluca inclined his head. "I am."

The old woman turned her gaze on Hannah, who flushed even redder.

"Interesting," was all she said. Then she bustled in farther to sweep up a squealing, giddy Dominic in her arms, and carried him off into the back room.

"That is my neighbor and landlady," Hannah told him when they were alone again. "Cinzia Pisanelli. She's a godsend. And a good friend. And as far as Dominic is concerned, she's his grandmother."

"What of his actual grandparents?"

Hannah smiled, though he thought it seemed a bit

tight. Forced. "He's never met them. They're in Nebraska, after all."

And before he could reply to that, she was on her feet, and then moving around the room, picking up toys, and neatening things. When there was nothing left to sort out, she turned back to him, her hands on her hips.

"Am I fired?" she demanded, with that directness that made so many people claim they disliked Americans. But Antonluca prized straightforwardness in most circumstances. Even if hers was...bracing. "Or are we going into work today?"

"You are thinking about work at a time like this?"

She tilted her head a bit to one side and looked at him as if the words he used made no sense. "I think about work all the time. That's why I'm good at it. And I do not have an empire, like some. I have to work. It's how I take care of Dominic."

"That is not something you will need to worry about again," he said then, surprised.

And maybe a bit too intently, because she frowned.

"If that is supposed to make me feel better, it doesn't," she told him.

"I don't know how you are supposed to feel, Hannah. I don't know how *I* am supposed to feel. Do you think there is a manual for this situation we are in? If so, I would love to see it. But do you really think that fussing over a Christmas market will make any of this better?"

"I can't answer that for you." She said that simply. Quietly. It made him feel small, somehow, that she could stand there before him and simply *exude* dignity. "I suppose you will do whatever it is you need to do. But I warn you, I will also do what I have always done, which is to take care of my child."

"Our child," he corrected her.

Softly, but with heat behind it.

He wasn't sure if he expected her to argue or not, but all she did was incline her head, her gaze on his.

And Antonluca felt something in him loosen. A knot he hadn't even known was there. Something tight and hard that he hadn't understood was buried down beneath too many layers to count, deep in his chest.

Yet Hannah made it go away, that easily.

He would have considered it magic, if only it didn't ache.

But what he knew too well was that there was precious little magic in this world. He had experienced it himself, when he was so young that he should have seen magic everywhere. He had lived too many lives already, that was the thing.

Antonluca had never intended to bring a child into this world. His own childhood had been too rough for him to imagine continuing on in that fashion. Or at all.

He never meant to do it, but he had. Just as he had taken no precautions last night, either, like a fool.

Or maybe…not such a fool, now that he considered it.

Because Antonluca had never planned or wanted to

become a father. But now that it turned out he was one, he knew exactly what it was he had to do.

And *would* do.

Whether Hannah liked it or not.

CHAPTER SEVEN

"WE MUST GET MARRIED," Antonluca informed her, as if issuing a decree.

But since it was *impossible* that he had said such a thing, all Hannah could do was stare at him.

"What?"

That was not the sort of polished reply she was known for, but it was all she had.

It was the week before Christmas. They had been running around all day, preparing the hotel for its grand tree-lighting ceremony tonight. Hannah had expected that Antonluca would make things difficult for her after he'd discovered Dominic's existence. She'd expected... retaliation, perhaps. Or at least some version of coldness or pettiness in case she was tempted to forget that he thought she deliberately betrayed him.

Last time around, despite the night they'd shared, he'd had her fired and blacklisted.

Lest she forget.

But this time around, with much higher stakes, he had disconcerted her by acting like a consummate professional. If she hadn't known only too well that he had only found out that he was a father a handful of days before, she wouldn't have had the slightest idea that anything had occurred in his personal life. She was certain no one else had noticed any change in him at all.

He is as unchanging as the sea, Léontine had murmured at some point.

The sea is ever-changing, Hannah had replied. *That's the whole point of it, surely.*

Yet it remains the sea, replied the concierge, with a faint shrug.

Hannah had thought about that a lot.

Now he'd walked into her office, taken the chair that he normally did, and then come out with this...absurdity.

Hannah studied him, taking in the way his gray eyes glittered and the way he tilted that strong jaw of his, as if he was prepared to get belligerent if necessary.

There was no reason that should make her *shiver*, she chastised herself. Particular not in the absence of anything like fear.

He had taken to coming over every morning before work. Each time he did, it made more and more of Hannah's heart hurt, because Dominic just loved him. Dominic couldn't get enough of him. Add to that the inescapable fact that Dominic looked just like his father and it *did something* to Hannah.

It made her feel connected to Antonluca in a way she knew, logically, she wasn't. It made her daydream about becoming a family in a real sense when she knew that was something several degrees more than simply foolish. She was, in the end, really not much more than a simple girl who was good at hospitality. *He*, on the other hand, was...Antonluca Aniello.

Then again, she thought now, maybe foolishness was going around.

"I believe that you heard me," Antonluca said. His voice was measured, but nothing about his expression or that glint in his gaze offered anything that suggested calm rationality.

She opted not to examine too closely the way that expression made everything inside of her...seem to *gleam*.

Just as she did not permit herself to remember that look that Antonluca had worn on his face after he'd seen Dominic for the first time. Or the way they'd crashed together after that, in such a bright, blistering fury—

"I did hear you," she conceded, because that was better than letting that memory sweep her away. "But I assumed I must have misunderstood. What on earth would make you think that *marriage* was a good idea?"

Antonluca gazed back at her without comprehension. "We have a child."

"Yes," she said, and Hannah had to shove aside the wellspring of emotion that wanted to flood her then, with all this *we*. *We* have a child, he'd said.

As if they were that family she'd always wished she had—

But she had to stop doing this to herself. *She had to*. It was self-preservation at this point.

She cleared her throat. "We have a child, but we didn't

have to be married to make him and we don't have to be married now, either."

"I would like my child to have my name," he told her, and even though those gray eyes of his glittered even more than before, if anything, his voice got smoother. Calmer.

Or maybe what it was, she thought as it seemed to expand inside of her, was *implacable*.

"If I had known you were having my child in the first place," he said in that same voice, so it seemed that even his gaze was a bit darker, then, "I would have insisted upon it before he was born."

"You would have *insisted*," she echoed.

"My child should have every possible protection that my name offers," Antonluca continued in that same calm, smooth manner. Yet with every syllable, it was as if more steel was infused into the words.

She stared back at him and realized that she hadn't moved since he'd started speaking. It was as if she *couldn't*. It was very much as if she'd frozen solid, but that was only her body. Inside, her emotions were running wild.

He wanted to *marry* her.

Except…it wasn't really her he wanted to marry, was it. Marrying her was a means to an end. This was all about Dominic. This had nothing to do with her at all.

And Hannah was torn, because part of her was fiercely glad. This was how she had felt about Dominic from the moment she'd finally come to understand what was happening to her body. She had vowed that she would protect her baby as fully and as selflessly as she knew how, and if she didn't know how, she'd learn.

But the other part of her, the part that could still feel Antonluca's hot, hard mouth on hers, and the way he had surged deep inside of her as if he had always belonged there, was...less glad.

An alarm sounded on her phone then, and it was like being released from a spell. She looked away from him, saw the message on her lock screen, and blew out a breath.

"I will take your...*proposal* under advisement," she said, trying her best not to sound too emotional. Or too anything, really. "But it's time for me to go make sure the tree lighting ceremony is going on without a hitch."

She stood up in a rush, gathered her things as best she could, and when he stood, too, she almost expected him to reach out and put his hand on her—

Maybe she only wished he would.

But he didn't.

Hannah found herself a little more emotional than planned as she made her way out into the main lobby. The guests had trickled in by now and the lobby was full, with holiday music playing in the background while the staff bustled around dispensing sweet treats—all from various Christmases around the world, from gingerbread men to Florentines to *pfeffernuesse* and more—and filling glasses with sparkling wine.

She was happy, immediately, that there was too much

to do for her to sink too deeply into the mess inside of her, because she had the feeling that once she did, there would be no climbing back out.

It was not until later, after each and every evergreen that they'd set up for this festival was lit and carolers sang before the grand fireplace, singing in at least five languages, that she found herself tucked in a corner and finally able to think about the fact that Antonluca Aniello, the man who had rocked her world entirely in New York and was the father of her son, *had proposed to her.*

Well, she corrected herself with perhaps the faintest hint of something like bitterness—or perhaps it was simple disappointment—*that isn't strictly true.*

It hadn't been a proposal. It had been a demand and it hadn't had much, if anything, to do with her.

Try as she might, she couldn't seem to get past that.

All night, she hadn't been able to really enjoy herself here, when this was truly one of her favorite nights of the year. It was even better this year, because the hotel was full and the guests were almost universally delighted. Hannah should have been floating on cloud nine.

Instead, she found herself returning again and again to a simple truth that she didn't want to face. Namely, that she was far more of a romantic than she'd ever thought she was.

Because there was a part of her that almost wished she'd never found out who that man in New York was. Now that she had—now that she knew—she could no longer pull out that night to escape into when she had a need for it. It was no longer her safe place, her happy place.

She'd used it as exactly that for years.

And she could admit, standing here listening to a glorious rendition of "O Holy Night" that some part of her was mourning that loss. Deeply.

Though not completely, because there had been so much gained, too. She was happy that the truth was out. She had expected it to be painful, and it had been—it was—but it had been painful to carry a baby to term and have him alone, so she supposed there was no way out of this without some measure of pain.

And as far she could tell, Antonluca understood that.

It didn't mean he was happy about it, but after that first night, there had been little talk of *betrayal*.

Another truth was that she enjoyed spending time with him.

She had discovered, to her surprise, that they were an excellent team. Whether he had originally planned to stay here this long or not, she had found that he was an excellent person to bounce ideas off. If he didn't know the answer to something, he knew how to find it, and always went about looking for it in intriguing ways.

Before Antonluca had found out about Dominic, Hannah had already been wrestling with the fact that she'd known him so *carnally*, so *physically* once. And then so *intellectually* these past few weeks.

It was like she only knew the man in puzzle pieces.

And now he wanted her to put them all together into a form that didn't make sense to her at all.

The carolers were singing a song about Joseph's heart, and Hannah was entirely too aware of her own. It beat too fast. It was much too fragile.

It *hurt*.

The trouble, she could acknowledge now that she was half-hidden by evergreen trees in a room filled with people who were not paying attention to her at all, was not that she didn't want to marry Antonluca.

On the contrary. Something inside of her leaped every time she considered it.

But Hannah didn't think that she could bear to marry a man who she knew didn't love her.

If she wanted more of that kind of life, she could move back to Nebraska.

She felt a helpless sort of laugh bubble up inside her at that, and when Léontine looked at her askance from beside her, Hannah made herself smile and lift her glass of sparkling wine. As if to suggest she was simply getting a little silly from all the bubbles.

Being profoundly French, Léontine nodded sagely, and carried on watching the carolers.

But Hannah finally understood something she'd been avoiding for a long time.

Not that Antonluca didn't love her. She was used to that, after all. And besides, as far she could tell, Antonluca not only didn't love her, he didn't love much of anything, so it wasn't likely to feel as personal as it did when it was her parents. Who clearly loved each other and Hannah's sister, but had used it all up by the time they got to her.

What was tragic about *this* situation was that she was deathly afraid, all of a sudden, that she'd fallen in love with him very much the way a stone falls off the side of a cliff. And worse, that she'd done so that very first night.

Possibly the very first moment she had looked over and been caught so completely, so inescapably, in that grave gaze of his.

And for once, she didn't shy away from that thought inside of her, the way she'd been doing at the faintest hint of it. She made herself breathe through it instead. She let it settle.

And then something else occurred to her. She remembered—as perhaps she always had, and had always convinced herself to ignore, push away, deny—that she had heard about this village from him.

That she and her mystery man had lain together in a tangle in that hotel bed, and one of the few things he'd told her was about a picture-perfect village in the hills of Tuscany, where the houses were ancient and bristled about on an old hill, there was a castle in the distance, and there were cypress trees on all sides, like guardian angels.

It had been Antonluca all along.

Hannah felt *hollowed out* by this realization.

What a terrible fool she'd been. What a terrible fool she was.

The next day, she made her dutiful call home to Nebraska, a habit she wasn't sure why she insisted on keeping. And as her parents talked, somehow managing to make it seem as if their very small lives doing the same small things they'd always done were somehow more virtuous and worthy of respect than anything Hannah could possibly be doing—off in Italy with what anyone else would agree was a high-level, exciting sort of job—she found herself getting more and more...not *angry*. That was too sharp.

Still, something was bubbling away inside of her and getting more insistent until finally, when they paused in the middle of a typical recitation of what was happening in their lives—which was in no way different from any other week, or any other year, because their implication was always that it should have been good enough for Hannah if it was good enough for them—she cracked a little bit.

She wasn't proud, but she did.

"I have some news, actually," she found herself saying, before they could recite the menu at the local diner where they liked to go on Tuesdays. She was standing at her window while Dominic and Cinzia were playing in the lane outside, bundled up against the cold, both red-cheeked and laughing.

"Let me guess," said her mother with sniff. "You had some or other exciting promotion, no doubt."

And it wasn't new, but never failed to amaze Hannah how they could take things that ought to have been, if not good or thrilling, at least neutral. Who *wouldn't* want a promotion? Why would that be something worthy of the disdain she heard in her mother's voice?

But she shook that off. "Not a promotion, no," Hannah said, the overly cheery voice she assumed whenever speaking to her parents, because she'd learned long ago that letting them see that she was upset not only didn't change anything, it made *her* feel worse. "Dominic's father and I have reconnected." There was nothing but silence and she already hated herself for bringing this up, but she forged ahead anyway. "He wants to marry me."

And surely, at last, she'd hit upon a thing they actually wanted. She waited for some expressions of excitement. Or at least a gesture toward a positive reaction.

Her mother sniffed. That was all.

After a while, her father sighed. "If he really wanted to do the right thing," he said, as if Hannah was not very bright and he had to talk down to her to get her to understand how very not bright she was, "it wouldn't have taken him this long, would it?"

And for entirely too long after they hung up, Hannah stayed where she was, staring out the window but not seeing anything. Or maybe it was that she was seeing too much, and all of it clearly, for once. When she could finally bring herself to move, she pulled on her warm coat and stamped into her cozy boots, then went outside to join Cinzia and Dominic in the fresh, bracing afternoon.

Dominic was running around in gleeful circles,

shrieking with joy. It was impossible to look at a happy child like him and do anything but smile, so that was what Hannah did.

Her son was pure joy, and she took terrific pride in loving him fiercely, and absolutely.

Because over her dead body would *he* ever question whether or not he was loved.

"Another pleasant call home, I gather," said Cinzia from beside her.

Hannah shook her head and didn't get into it, because what was there to say? It shamed her, if she was honest. Because surely there had to be something deeply unlovable in her if not a single member of her family could manage to muster up even the littlest bit of common courtesy. There had to be something terrible about her that she just couldn't see.

And if her friend couldn't see it, Hannah certainly didn't want to be the one to tell her.

"I told them some news that they were not particularly interested in," she said instead of dissecting all the weary sighs and little digs. But she smiled at her friend. "I think you might be, though. Dominic's father wishes to marry me."

The old woman eyed her for a moment. "By *Dominic's father*, just to be perfectly clear, we are discussing the *maestro* himself, are we not? Antonluca Aniello, local *castello* dweller and currently the owner of La Paloma."

"Yes," Hannah said quietly. "You've met."

They stood there together, watching as Dominic found a stick that delighted him and started up an imaginary sword fight right there in the middle of the lane.

"You do not seem overcome with joy at this news," Cinzia pointed out, rather diplomatically.

"I just…" Hannah shook her head. "He doesn't want to marry me, just to be clear. He wants to marry the mother of his child so that his son will have his name. Let's not romanticize this."

After his epic sword fight, Dominic looked to be approaching a level of excitement that would likely tip over too quickly into a meltdown, so Hannah and Cinzia moved to each take one of his hands and set off on a more sedate walk down the lane, the better to avert disaster.

For a time, as they walked, Cinzia was quiet. When they got to the bottom of the lane and turned back, Hannah picked Dominic up and settled him on her hip. He was already sleepy, and he rested his head on her shoulder, pressing his face into her neck.

Hannah breathed him in, and felt her load lighten that easily.

Only then did Cinzia comment. "The man is not simply a gift horse with a mouth you could look into all day, and happily," she pointed out. "He ticks every box. He's outrageously attractive. You should hear the women in the village swoon and flutter over the very *thought* of him when attractive men are easy enough to come by." She waved a gloved hand. "This is Italy. *Ovviamente*."

Hannah laughed. "*Ma certo*," she replied, because she knew better than to argue about the riches of Italy with Italians.

"Antonluca Aniello is not any run-of-the-mill Italian man," Cinzia continued. "He is also wealthy beyond measure. He can provide for both you and Dominic, forever."

Hannah blew out a breath. "I understand. I know that. But…"

"But?"

"Is that enough?" Hannah shook her head, and found that Cinzia's intent gaze made her feel…raw. Too vulnerable. "Surely a marriage should be something more than simply…convenient."

"Should it?" Cinzia shrugged. "But who's to say that convenience cannot be the gateway to something marvelous?"

"He doesn't love me, Cinzia," Hannah said, baldly. She caught her friend's gaze, then looked away. "He doesn't love me. He doesn't pretend to."

They walked on, the only sound between them the wind rustling through the hills and the fields and the church bells in the distance. When they reached the front of their cottages, Cinzia turned to her again.

"You must do as you see fit," she counseled Hannah, and it seemed to Hannah that there was wisdom pouring out of her kind eyes and those lines in her lovely face. "But I will say this. A wise woman uses the tools she has, and fashions precisely what she wants with them."

Hannah shook her head, holding Dominic tight. "I don't know what that means."

The older woman's gaze was knowing. "It is not as if the man is immune to you, is he?"

And Hannah thought about little else once she put Dominic down for his nap. She answered emails and a few calls from the hotel. She moved around the cottage, but she was thinking about that castle on the hill.

She continued to think about it the following day, when she and Antonluca did their daily walk-through of the Christmas Market and then put their heads together over sets of figures and projections.

And, she thought, *as long as I can work, I can survive anything.*

That was the key, she thought as they sat close together and had a very dry conversation about revenue and occupancy. As long as she could do her job, she could make everything else work. She'd already done it once, as a single mother in a foreign country. She could do it again, and this time with the added benefit of being a very rich man's wife.

If La Paloma was any indication, that was its own cottage industry.

That night, he walked her out to her car in the staff forecourt, as had become his custom. There were flurries of snow spiraling down all around them, though not sticking to the ground. And when they reached her vehicle, he insisted on waiting there at the driver's side window until the car was properly warm and the windows defrosted.

He stood there and insisted that she wait until he was satisfied that she could drive safely.

And something about it pierced her straight through.

Possibly because it was sad, really, that she couldn't think of anyone else in her life who had taken this kind of care of her, not so consistently. Cinzia was a wonder, and they were truly friends, but Hannah also paid her rent. So really it was only Antonluca.

Sadder still, the kind of care he was taking with her here was so matter-of-fact. She felt certain she could have been anyone. He was simply being polite to the mother of his child.

But something about that was soothing, too.

Because she couldn't really mourn what she'd never had, could she? And if he took care of her like this, on a snowy night when he could as easily have done nothing at all, then certainly he would take care of his child.

He would insist upon it.

And if Hannah and Dominic could depend on that, well. That was no small thing.

There, in the dark, with only her headlights against the night and the snow dancing all around, it felt expansive.

Something close enough to miraculous.

"Very well, then," Antonluca said in his grave way, apparently deciding that her windshield was clear enough. "I will see you in the morning."

"All right," she agreed. But he was looking down at her and that gray gaze seemed to be as much inside her as in front of her.

And this time, instead of simply falling off the side of a cliff and plummeting against her will into a life she couldn't have imagined in advance, she could decide. She could *choose* the fall, and that felt powerful.

So she did.

She reached over and she put her hand on the sleeve of his coat.

"Yes," she said.

"Yes?" he repeated.

She swallowed, and asked herself if she meant it. If she really, truly wanted this. But she did.

Hannah jumped, and it was much, much better than falling. That was clear at once. This way, it felt like she was flying.

"Yes, Antonluca," she said, with all the gravity the moment deserved, though her heart had wings and she let them unfurl, where only she could see them. "I will marry you."

CHAPTER EIGHT

ANTONLUCA APPROACHED HIS upcoming nuptials the way he did everything in this world, which was also the *only* way he knew how to do anything.

Meaning, he treated it like business.

And he was deliberately as cold and as calculating as possible in all things when it concerned his business, because that was how a street kid who came from nothing became an international phenomenon.

He quickly decided that there was no point in inviting their families. Antonluca and Hannah were becoming a family thanks to Dominic, and surely that was enough. And he didn't have very many friends, either. Friendships were the sorts of things that were developed when a person had free time, and he'd never had any. Certainly not when he was younger, and could have used some friends. Back then he'd had work and his siblings, that was all.

But then he'd become very famous and very rich, very fast, and had quickly discovered that he could not possibly trust anyone who cozied up to him once that happened. They didn't want *him*. They wanted the image they had of him in their heads and those two things never matched.

If he really took the time to consider it closely, that had likely been a huge part of why he'd liked Hannah so much, and so instantaneously, in New York. It had been very clear that she had no idea who he was. Not the faintest inkling.

For the first time in as long as he could remember, someone had simply...liked him for him.

It still made Antonluca hard when he remembered it.

Then again, so did the memory of her delicate, gloved hand on his arm and her face tilted up toward his as she sat in that car of hers that night. There had been snow in the air and the faint sound of music in the distance from the hotel lobby. He had thought to himself that she had never looked more beautiful, this one long night that had become so much more.

And then she had agreed to become his wife.

There was very little about Hannah that did not arouse him, which was something Antonluca found he was more comfortable admitting now.

Because she was going to become his wife. *She'd agreed.*

So he set about making certain that she didn't have time to change her mind. He didn't want to involve his siblings, because he wasn't interested in their opinions on this matter, and they would certainly wish to give them anyway. There were no friends to gather near, which he decided was a blessing.

What he had, in lieu of those things, was a great deal of money, a lovely old chapel that had been built in his castle when the residents needed to pray over the deaths caused by many ancient battles, and the ability to obtain, within twenty-four hours, a special license to marry at will.

All he needed then was a priest to perform the ceremony.

"This is very unusual," the priest tutted reprovingly when Antonluca called on him in person, special license in hand.

"It seems to me that all the churches in the diocese could use repairs," Antonluca replied, with a vague wave of his hand toward the whole of the village outside, and the rolling hills beyond with their dusting of white. "Perhaps they have roofs that date back a few wars. Perhaps they could use plumbing from at least the last century or so. Modern conveniences are so helpful, do you not think, in allowing the faithful to concentrate on their eternal souls instead of historic irritants."

"Love is a beautiful thing," the priest said to that, with a beneficent smile. As Antonluca had been certain he would. "Especially at this time of year, is it not?"

The only slight wrinkle in all of this efficiency was that Hannah did not seem quite as delighted as Antonluca felt she should.

It seemed to him that she had taken some sort of step back even as she had agreed to the wedding, and he didn't like it. But he didn't want to risk discussing it and thereby ruining their forward momentum. He therefore decided that what he needed to do was keep his eyes on the prize.

He had to marry her. He had to make certain that she was his and do what was necessary to claim his son, too. Everything else could be handled later.

Once Hannah was his.

"We will get married tonight," he told her one morning at La Paloma, with no preamble or attendant fanfare.

It seemed to him that Hannah took much too long looking up from her computer screen and even longer to meet his gaze.

When she did, he thought her gaze was unduly measured.

"Thank you for informing me," she said.

Very calmly. *Too* calmly, to his mind.

Antonluca had the nearly ungovernable urge to vault over the desk, get his hands on her, and remind her how easy it was for neither one of them to feel the least bit *calm* about anything, not while they were busy tearing each other apart.

Because they were so damned good at tearing each other apart.

"We will go back to the castle after work," he told her in the same tone, as if delivering a list of demands. "Cinzia will be waiting and she will have Dominic with her, of course."

At that, Hannah's mouth curved, and Antonluca felt something flood through him that could only be relief—but he didn't want to admit that. He didn't want to accept that it took only the faintest smile from her to make him feel soothed. To make him feel…

Well. Anything at all.

"Dominic will be very excited," Hannah said then, still smiling. "He's always wanted to visit a castle."

He didn't want to categorize the feelings that charged through him then. He didn't want to believe he was capable of that kind of softening. His voice was unnecessarily gruff when he replied. "Then he will be even more excited to live in one."

Her green eyes flashed as they met his and he expected her to argue, or at least respond with something other than that calm, quiet *competence* of hers, but she didn't. He watched the column of her throat move as she swallowed. Carefully.

Everything about Hannah was so *careful* and it made him…want to mess her up a little. Just enough.

"Then he will be the luckiest boy alive, clearly," she replied.

Without inflection.

Very much as if she knew that she was getting under his skin.

He believed she did.

And it was closer still to Christmas now. There were a thousand different things going on in the hotel, all calculated to make the guests feel as if they were in a fantasy version of home, whatever that meant to them.

This was why Antonluca did not shadow her when

she left him in the office later that morning. Hannah had been asked to personally supervise a particular VIP group of guests into Florence for the day. It was but one of the services the hotel offered to those who settled in and made a holiday out of their stay. Excursions to anywhere with the same luxurious attention to detail available at La Paloma, all with the same casual presentation of that luxury that made a certain kind of remarkably wealthy person feel downright cozy.

And as he was one of those people, he should know.

He waited for her later that evening. He sat in her sterile office, wondering why she had no pictures of Dominic on her walls or her desktop. It was tempting to imagine that she'd been hiding the baby from him that way, but he didn't think so. According to all reports and his own observations here, Hannah was a consummate professional in all things.

Too much so, to his mind.

Still, he had discovered today that he could be, too, as he'd stayed at the hotel and had answered many of the calls that would normally be within Hannah's purview. It was a far cry from the loud, busy kitchens that had defined the height of his career, but Antonluca had enjoyed himself all the same.

There was something deeply satisfying about solving the guests' various problems in ways that made them happier than before. He supposed it was not so different from the kind of customer service he liked to offer in his restaurants—but he wasn't sure he'd ever been so personally involved in the process.

It was a surprise to him that he quite liked it.

He was mulling that over when Hannah came marching into the office, bringing the scent of snow from outside with her. She stopped dead when she saw him, and he thought, once again, that it took her a moment too long to produce that polite smile of hers.

"How did things go?" she asked, no trace of any hesitation in her voice. "I was delighted to see that the hotel did not crumble in my absence."

But she smiled a little wider to show she was kidding.

"I didn't know how I would like it," he told her. "If you want to know the real truth, I would have told you that I had no other skills than cooking."

"On the contrary," she assured him. "Léontine made a point of coming to speak to me when I came in. She wanted to make sure that I knew that you handled everything beautifully and impressed the entire concierge staff. In case you were looking for validation."

He was Antonluca Aniello. It was never his goal to achieve external validation. It was not required, because such was his talent.

On the other hand, he found himself quite pleased indeed that he received such rave reviews. And from such an unlikely source as the ferocious French concierge who made *edginess* seem plush and soft.

He did not know how to express that, so instead he cleared his throat and said, "How was your trip?"

"It went well," Hannah replied.

She moved past him, being very careful that no part of either one of them brushed against the other, though he felt certain she was as aware of him as he was of her. That awareness buzzed around them and lit him up inside. She went around behind her desk and stacked up some papers, exchanging them with whatever she had in her bag.

And she kept up the easy, professional talk as she did it. "It always surprises me how much members of certain tax brackets, where the air is always rarified, truly enjoy pretending that they are normal people for a day."

"Wealth is isolating," Antonluca replied, without realizing he meant to say such a thing. He blinked, then continued. "That isn't a complaint, I hasten to add. But I am not at all surprised that a great many wealthy people like to create feelings of authenticity here and there."

"It was certainly that," Hannah said. "If authenticity comes with the ability to wander about a crowded city as if it was theirs alone while receiving priority treatment at every turn."

"For them, it does," he replied.

She was still wearing her coat as she straightened from her desk. He noticed it because it fell open over the dress she was wearing, a lovely winter white that she'd been wearing earlier and seemed particularly perfect, today.

For a long moment, they gazed at each other.

And Antonluca did not know what to say, so he simply held out his hand and waited.

He thought that a clock was ticking as he waited for her to put her hand in his, but there was no ticking clock in this office. It turned out, he discovered after a few moments, that it was merely his heart. Keeping time. Keeping him company, until, with a deep breath that he could actually feel in every part of him, she slipped her hand into his.

Then he stood there without moving, because this reminded him too much of that first night in New York. Her delicate-looking but surprisingly strong hand in his. That compelling green gaze of hers and the way the air seemed to change between them.

And he was certain that he meant to say something, but all he could do was feel the full circle of this. That moment to this, like a straight line. As if there had never been any deviation. As if they'd always been meant to come directly here.

He felt something inside him, like a deep hard pull from the deepest part of him. Some kind of well springing up from part of him that he wasn't sure he even knew.

"Hannah," he began.

She squeezed his hand and her smile changed, but he couldn't have said how. Only that it did.

"Shall we go get married, then?" she asked, a shade or two too brightly.

And he was...not *frustrated*, not quite that as she

pulled her hand back and stepped in front of him to head out of the office. Leaving him to trail behind her, watching as she nodded to all the staff as she headed out.

It occurred to him to wonder if she considered him, and their relationship, some kind of secret. Did she really think that she could marry him and no one would know?

Did she think they were not already the topic of speculation?

He was pondering this question as they stepped outside into the cold, and walked in silence through the dark.

"You do know that it will be impossible to hide the fact that you are marrying me and that Dominic is my son," he said, and didn't like that he could hear something like temper in his voice. He could only hope that she did not.

If she did she only glanced at him, then away. "I have no intention of hiding anything," she told him in that same maddeningly *even* way. "But I also think that nothing good can come of rubbing everyone's face in it. I assumed that we would simply carry on as usual and keep our private life to ourselves."

That was more or less how Antonluca preferred to live his life, so he could not have said why it was that hearing her say such a thing...rankled.

She went to keep walking down toward the forecourt where most of the staff kept their cars, but he stopped her. Then he inclined his head toward his Range Rover.

It sat, gleaming and shiny, in the owner's spot in the circular drive that swept up to the hotel's main entrance.

"We will take my car, I think," he told her, with perhaps more intensity than the matter of transportation required. "I do not think it will be necessary for you to drive that questionable Fiat of yours again."

"I like that questionable Fiat." There was a frown between her eyes. "It has served me well."

"It is unsafe," he replied coolly.

He opened the passenger door to the Range Rover, and beckoned for her to get in. He thought there was some resistance there. In the way that she frowned at him. In the fact that she did not respond to his safety concerns.

But in the end, she swung herself into the seat and settled there, gazing out the window as if she was the very picture of serenity.

What he could not figure out was why he did not feel that as a win.

"I thought you preferred to walk, even in the cold," she said once he swung into the driver's seat, started the car, and began to drive.

"I do," he said, and was surprised as he said it to discover that he truly meant it. He'd begun his walking as some form of penance, perhaps. Or acknowledgment. And maybe it was both. But he had also come to enjoy the time alone in his head.

Something in him kicked at him, urging him to tell her that, but he didn't.

"Tonight, however, it is our wedding night," he said gruffly, in case she'd forgotten that. "Even I know better than to take a bride tramping across the field in the cold."

And when she didn't reply, he glanced over, and saw what looked like the most real smile he'd seen today on her lips as she gazed out the window.

This time, it felt like a win. It felt like winning a grand prize, in fact.

He drove into the village and then out again, then down into the fields once more only to climb back up toward the castle. The lights were blazing tonight, and he supposed that was more of an announcement to the village than anything else could have been. Since he preferred, generally speaking, to minimize that sort of thing.

A candle in the dark and the dream of former kings, is that it? one of the old men in the village had asked him once, during a break from the bocce tournament.

A man is nothing but his dreams, old man, Antonluca had replied.

Though he hadn't believed that, not then. Tonight he pulled into the old gates and across the stone slabs that had once been some kind of courtyard. And then he led the mother of his child, this woman who would soon become his wife, into the castle that was his.

And now hers, too.

There was a part of him that wanted to go back in

time to find that street kid he'd been and tell him that it was all going to work out. And for the best.

Because this was the dream he'd never dared dream, not back when he didn't know if he'd manage to keep his siblings fed.

Inside the grand hall, Dominic and Cinzia were waiting for them. The little boy came charging over to his parents as they came in, tossing himself at Hannah—and then put Antonluca's heart at risk by doing the same to him.

The quicker they married, he thought fiercely, the better.

He ushered them all into the same room where he'd entertained his brother and that weaselly man Rocco had produced out of nowhere. Until this very night, this had been one of the very few furnished rooms in the castle, outside his kitchens.

The priest waited there, smiling benevolently, and after introductions were made, they all walked together through the castle and out once more into the courtyard. Once outside, they hurried through the cold toward the tiny chapel that was tucked into one corner.

"A beautiful example of medieval fortification," the priest said to Antonluca as they walked. "I'm delighted that you have kept the whole of this *castello* so pristine. Such attention to historical detail."

"Historical detail is my passion," Antonluca replied dryly, and wasn't sure why he'd even done such a thing until he saw the way Hannah's lips quirked.

And in that moment, he had the distinct, lowering impression that he—world-famous, too wealthy to ever worry about poverty again—felt like every teenage boy who had ever existed. Because he understood that he would do absolutely anything to entertain this woman.

He had just proved it.

That made him feel almost dizzy. It was disorienting in every way, so he was pleased to enter the chapel and have them all cluster together there at the ancient altar, because that meant that this was happening.

He was sure that, once it did, he would stop being *victimized* by all these *feelings*.

The priest made a meal of it, but that was only to be expected.

"Antonluca," he intoned, "do you take Hannah, here present, for your lawful wife according to the rite of our holy mother, the Church?"

Antonluca was the one who had wanted a religious ceremony, not merely a civil one, to make certain these bindings between them stayed put. And now that he was standing in a drafty old chapel, he wished they could hurry it all up.

But first there were these vows. *"Lo voglio,"* he growled. "I do."

Then found himself on tenterhooks as he waited for the priest to ask Hannah the same question. An eternity passed, it seemed to him, as he waited for her to answer. As her solemn green gaze held his, then moved to the priest.

"Yes," she said, her voice clear. "I do."

After that, the service was otherwise swift and to the point.

Or Antonluca thought it was, in any case, having not attended any weddings before.

He repeated the words that he was told to repeat. He listened as Hannah did the same. He held her hands in his as they said ancient words and followed old rites to bind themselves together into one.

And then, at last, he slid a dramatic emerald that matched her eyes onto her hand, then followed it up with the matching band that slid in tight to the emerald and made the entire set look more intricate, more unique. He handed her the ring that he had selected for himself and there was something shocking about how deeply he liked the fact that in pushing that ring onto his finger, she was claiming him, too.

That understanding seemed to flash between them then. Scared and sweet.

And then the priest pronounced them husband and wife. At last.

Dominic was giggling with Cinzia, who was murmuring to him in a low voice, but all that Antonluca could focus on was pulling Hannah closer to him. She had shed her coat when they'd entered the chapel and she wore the same simple white gown she had been wearing all day.

But to him, there was no more beautiful wedding gown in existence. Because no other gown would have her in it, and that was really the beginning and the end of all of this for him.

She tipped her head back. He cupped her jaw with his hand and leaned in.

And he remembered then, when they had stepped outside onto a busy New York street but neither of them had noticed all the cars and people. Instead he had done something very much like this, his palm against the side of her face.

He thought that she was remembering it, too, given the way her eyes darkened.

Just like that, he fit his mouth to hers.

Carefully. Deliberately.

And it was the restraint that almost killed him. The restraint that became something like reverence, because their child was here and there was a priest beside them and this was no time to give in to all that flame and fury that he could feel blazing all around them.

There was only this claiming. Only this surge of certainty that he could feel his bones, his flesh, his greedy cock.

When they separated, her eyes seemed to brighten and her lips trembled, and when she looked away, he let her.

Because he felt as shaken as she looked.

They trooped back into the castle then. There was a celebratory drink and a small meal with the grinning priest, and then Cinzia toted Dominic off for what she called a sleepover party at her house.

The little boy was thrilled. He told his mother all about it, in his high-pitched, excited, not entirely comprehensible way and then told Antonluca about it, too.

When Cinzia left, the priest followed, and he found himself alone at last with his wife.

Antonluca could feel a wild hungering within him, unlike any he had ever known.

But he held it in check. He let the quiet of the castle settle in him. Then he turned to look at Hannah, who was standing there by the fire. Gazing into the flames as if they were sharing their secrets with her.

"I know I have known Dominic only a short while," he said in a low voice. "But it feels…"

"Yes," she agreed. "The minute I laid eyes on him it was as if I had always known him. As if I had been waiting for all my life to meet him, and there he was."

He would not have found the words to say it in that way. Yet now that she had, it was as if she had unlocked that in him. That sense of recognition that he felt inside him, having only very little to do with how the boy *looked*.

"I want to thank you," Antonluca said, stiff and formal and strange, but there was no helping it. "You could have made me fight for this. I am honored."

She tipped her head slightly to one side, her gaze still on the flames that danced in the grate. "I hope I can always be counted on to do what is best for Dominic."

At another time, he decided, he would dig into why he found that so…*wrong*. Why it made his skin seem to shrink against his bones while something dark settled in his chest.

But not tonight.

"Welcome to my castle," he said instead. "The old men in the village call me their run-down king. I suppose that makes you their queen."

And it was clear that this was the exact right note to hit, because she smiled. It even seemed like a real smile. When he extended his hand, she came to him and took it immediately, and that was good. He could feel her heat, her grip as he led her out of the living room, and guided her all around the castle itself.

The grand tour, such as it was.

"I'm not trying to sound disparaging," she said as they climbed the stairs, after walking around the main level, which was mostly the room they'd already been and the kitchens that had been the only thing he'd insisted upon renovating before moving in. And, of course, a handful of rooms that stood empty, all stone and starlight tonight. "But I will say that I was expecting lavish corridors of marble. Galleries filled with priceless works of art. Statues leaping out of every alcove, that sort of thing."

"I forget you are American," he said, though he smiled when he said it and she smiled back. "You are thinking of a palace, I think. There are many parts of history in which a stout stone wall could only be the province of self-proclaimed kings and they were used for the express purpose of holding off attackers and would-be replacements. A palace is much prettier, and usually less functional."

She wrinkled her nose, still smiling. "Marble can be perfectly functional, Antonluca. If you want it badly enough."

Antonluca found himself gazing at her, as close to a wide grin as he thought he'd ever come. He led her into the tower, climbing up the spiral stair and stopping just before the top, on a gated landing. He opened the door to show her what he'd had his staff do while she was in Florence today.

Hannah peered inside, her eyes wide. "*Oh*. This is Dominic's room." Her voice was laced with wonder. It made him feel like flying. "You've replicated it almost exactly."

"I want him to feel at home," Antonluca told her. Gruffly.

Then he led her up the last few steps to the expansive suite that took up the top of the tower. There was a sitting area with a separate room on that same level and a stair that led up even farther above. Unlike the rest of the castle, it was modernized and furnished and more, comfortable.

Hannah breathed out audibly when she saw it. "*This* is where you live," she said softly.

"You can take the room down here, if you wish it," he told her, because they hadn't discussed these things. It had seemed too fraught with peril, to Antonluca's mind.

As if talking about what their marriage might look like would make certain it never came to be.

But now they were good and truly married.

He still had hold of her hand, so he led her across the round space, and up the last spiral stair. There, at the very top of the tower, there were windows all around, and a modern sort of floating wall behind the bed that concealed a bathroom suite. And even at night, it was clear that there were views in every direction. As if all of Tuscany was theirs for the taking.

"Or," he said, not entirely sure why he couldn't seem to stop sounding so formal and strange, "we can share—"

But then it didn't matter, because Hannah catapulted herself into his arms.

The force of it surprised him, but he caught her in midair anyway. He held her there against his body as she kissed his face and wrapped her arms around his neck. He held her securely, so that finally—*finally*—he could really kiss her.

Not the way they had kissed in the chapel. This kiss was carnal. It was seeking, and filled with all of that wildfire that had always been theirs.

It was as hot as New York and as wild as the cottage and better than both.

He swung her up higher in his arms, and this was better than carrying her over some threshold. Because it was only a few steps across the room, and then he was laying her down on the bed and following her there.

Where, for the first time, he let himself settle in beside her and make certain to thoroughly kiss his wife.

Which was all he did.

Over and over and over again, until she began to beg. First softly. Then louder.

Then louder still, at which point, Antonluca laughed. And started over.

This time, he decided to slow down and enjoy every moment, every last second, because he'd spent entirely too long reliving the moments they'd already had.

It was better live. He wanted to revel in this, in her. In his *wife*.

He moved from the bed and pulled her to the very edge, then helped her pull her gown up over her head. He tossed it aside and made a deep, approving noise as he gazed at her. Without the gown, she was wearing nothing but one of those bustiers and only a scrap of lace between her legs.

"*Sei bellissima*," he managed to get out. "So damned beautiful."

He knelt down before her and without preamble, leaned in and pressed his open mouth to that V between her thighs. He sucked on her, hard, and she made a strangled noise in her throat, then bucked against him.

So he moved closer, settling her legs over his shoulders, and letting his teeth share this pleasure.

He ate at her until she was riding against him, pressing that softest part of her into his mouth. Then he used his hands to pull those panties away and lick his way into all that soft heat beneath.

Antonluca growled in approval as she broke apart, arching up into him with her arms thrown back over her head.

And as she sobbed out her pleasure, he moved back and shrugged his way out of his own clothes. Then he stretched out on the bed beside her, turned her over, and felt something in him kick, hard, when she wrapped herself around him and pulled him to her so he was on top.

"Please," she whispered.

And Antonluca was nothing if not obliging, so he reached between them to run his fingers through her dampness and then work his way deep inside of all that searing, molten heat.

She wrapped her legs around his waist and her arms around his neck, and there was something fierce and stark on her face as she began to move—undulating her hips and forcing him to sink in a little deeper.

He braced himself over her and sank as deep inside her as he could, and only then—only when they were both gasping at that thick, slick fit—did he begin to hammer in and out.

Over and over again at that same smooth, hard pace until he wasn't sure if either one of them was clinging to anything resembling sanity—because God help them both, this was almost *too* good. This was almost *too* intense.

This is Hannah, he reminded himself, *my wife*.

And he only realized that he'd said that out loud when she whispered back, "My husband."

That was when he lost control. Completely.

He clasped her close and she sobbed against his neck, even biting him as she began to shake all over again.

And he let himself go. He let himself pound into her, recklessly and heedlessly, and it felt so good that he heard himself shout out his pleasure as the flames consumed him.

Even better, he held her close as they both spun off into oblivion.

Because only here, skin to skin, was he entirely sure of her.

Only here, tangled together like this, did he feel connected to her—a part of her—at last.

CHAPTER NINE

AND THEN, SUDDENLY, Hannah found herself living in some strange little fairy tale.

She worked every day in a luxury hotel, where every room was a study in soaring elegance, exquisite fragrance, everything lush and welcoming. Christmas Eve was fast approaching and as if the hotel was its very own Advent calendar, every day they unveiled a little more sparkle. A little more glee.

Every night when she left the hotel in all its graceful splendor, she let the starkly beautiful man who was not quite a stranger drive her home through the magical hills of Tuscany to a bare-bones castle, all forbidding stone and echoing, empty rooms.

But like any other fairy tale, she knew better than to look too closely at all that starkness, at all those hints of disrepair. Because he was her baby's father. And more to the point, he was her husband.

And while his castle might have been cold and bare, there was nothing about the bed they shared that was anything but hot.

So hot, so blisteringly good, that Hannah often wondered if she was even the same woman she'd been before.

Because it had never occurred to her that the night they'd shared in New York City could be anything but an anomaly. She'd even felt smug about that, pleased because then there were no other, less transformative facts about him or them to concern herself with. There was no *mundane* when it came to one transformative night that she hadn't expected to repeat.

She had assumed that they would fall into a routine now that they were married, but they didn't.

He had not outdone himself in New York. It turned out. If anything, that night had only been the start. The faintest hint of what he could do and how they could come together and make that magic, that wildfire rush.

Within three days, Hannah understood things about her body that she'd never believed possible before, and Antonluca already knew each and every one of them.

In the morning, she would stand in the shower while he went to get Dominic up, and sometimes she even sobbed—but not because she was sad. But because she'd had no idea that it was possible to love another grown adult human this much, with her body as well as her heart.

And if she wasn't mistaken, the better part of her soul as well.

Hannah wasn't a complete fool. She was keenly aware

that they were on a fast track toward building out their family, though they had never discussed it. But did it require discussion? They both knew how Dominic had come into the world. Yet neither one of them protested when birth control wasn't used.

Again and again and again.

But then, she was just as capable of saying something as he was, and she wasn't a virgin any longer. Hannah knew exactly what could happen and likely would.

In not talking about it, they were both speaking pretty loudly, she thought.

The truth was, she was glad.

Maybe she'd spend her life regretting these dark outside, brightly lit within weeks in this rush to Christmas, but she doubted it.

Because he could have locked her away in a tower, as kings with castles were wont to do, but he hadn't. They were almost certainly making a future in these long nights, and Hannah thought he had to be as aware of it as she was.

And even if she did end up regretting this—this wild abandon, this glorious immolation—she found herself thinking that it would only be by the light of day. Come nightfall, when she was tucked up in her bed, locked away or not, she knew exactly what she would be dreaming about.

The slide of that huge, beautiful cock of his, deep inside her. The way he held her hips in his hands and guided her when he wanted to control the pace, the depth, and her reaction.

He was a demon, and he was some kind of archangel, and the contrast between their crisp and deliberate professionalism at work and the abandoned way they both succumbed to this fire between them in bed—

Maybe *regret* was the wrong thing to worry about. Maybe surviving this was going to be the challenge.

In many ways, she counseled herself each day, *nothing has changed. Everything is more or less the same.*

Mostly, she knew, because Antonluca had gone to great lengths to make certain that her transition from cottage to castle was easy as possible.

It was, once again, an indication that he was more thoughtful than she expected him to be. Or than anyone else ever had been. It made her heart ache a bit every time.

"And how goes this loveless marriage of yours?" Cinzia asked one morning.

The older woman came every day to the castle, conveyed by one of the largely invisible staff members that Antonluca had informed Hannah—stiffly—were there for her use.

I have long maintained a skeleton staff, if that, he had told her. *But you and Dominic deserve more care. They will be only too happy to do your bidding.*

Hannah had not known how to tell him that she did not know the first thing about *staff*. Not when it was to attend to her own needs. If they had been staff that she could direct to take care of hotel guests, that would have made sense to her. Staff for just…living?

Maybe she was more Nebraskan than she'd ever dreamed.

This morning, Cinzia had found them all in the kitchen, where Dominic had been eating his breakfast while Antonluca drank the bitter coffee he preferred and Hannah had a bit of toast. Because she liked toast, but also because it was something that she could prepare for herself, since it made her feel strange to ask staff members to wait on her like that.

Not to mention that the other adult who lived in this place was a world-renowned chef, though he acted as if he had never been inside a kitchen in all of his life. But that was a different issue—and one that felt like a minefield.

Hannah had decided that she was better off staying firmly anti-minefield for as long as she could.

Cinzia had watched as Antonluca had taken his leave, informing Hannah that he had meetings in London, but would be flying back that night. She'd watched as Antonluca had moved in and kissed her, deeply. As if they were alone.

And once he'd left, the older woman had made no bones about watching the way that Hannah flushed. Deep and long and very, very red.

Dominic was sitting on one of the high chairs at the counter, and started wiggling in a manner that suggested that he was moments away from flinging himself toward the kitchen floor. Hannah took that as an opportunity to take him down before he cracked his head open. She set him on the ground, with the added benefit that this gave her something to look at besides Cinzia.

"*Il primo amore non si scorda mai*," Cinzia said quietly. Hannah wasn't sure of the translation—something about first love cutting the deepest, she rather thought. "But this is a good thing, is it not?"

"I don't know what it is," Hannah replied, keeping her eyes on Dominic as he played with the chair leg, as if it had suddenly become deeply intriguing to him. "Maybe there's no point analyzing it. Maybe there's only living it and hoping for the best."

"Remember," her friend said, and her voice was so kind that Hannah found herself blinking back tears, "this is *your* marriage. *Your* family. Whatever happened before, with your parents or whatever his past might hold, you can choose to put it behind you. You can choose, if you like, to make something new instead."

"You say that as if you've never heard of ghosts." Hannah looked at her then, fighting the urge to wrap her arms around herself. "But this country is so old. You must be surrounded by them."

"There is never any shortage of ghosts, child," Cinzia told her with her wise, wide smile. "But here in Italy, we make friends with the things that haunt us. How else could life be so beautiful?"

Hannah found herself thinking about that all day.

That night, she put Dominic to bed in his castle room

that he liked so much that he sometimes asked to go sit in it at different points in the day, just to be in it. She read him an extra story and tucked him into the big boy bed he'd moved into when they'd come here. And then, when he was finally asleep, she found herself padding around the strange, empty old stone rooms like she was the ghost here, after all.

She got her book and went in by the fire, but if she read anything at all, she didn't know. Because the next thing she did know she was waking up to find Antonluca braced above her, a stern, arrested sort of look on his face as he gazed down at her curled up in his chair.

"When did you get home?" she asked.

His eyes seemed to darken at that, and the air between them seemed to thin. And Hannah understood that using the word *home* was loaded, here. In this bright fire of theirs where everything was a feeling and nothing was ever discussed outright.

She sat up straighter, rubbing her hands over her face, less sanguine than she wanted to be. Less in control of herself than she needed to be around this man.

My husband, she thought, and that word never failed to make her heart kick at her.

"I got in now," he told her.

And she wasn't sure that she could tell the difference between the appropriately remote boss he was at work and the man who stood before her now in yet another bespoke suit that made him look every bit as powerful as he was.

Or maybe she was tired of pretending they were two different men.

She uncurled herself from the depths of the chair, and it seemed to her that it took him a little too long to move back as she did.

But he did move. And then she was standing, and they were still too close, or that was what her body was telling her, anyway. Her heart was going wild beneath her ribs and she was sure that he could tell that she was flushed. Everywhere.

In all the places he liked to taste.

"You must be hungry," she said. When he only stared at her, she shook her head. "What is it? You keep looking at me as if…?"

His mouth curved, but she was not sure that she would call it a smile. "I apologize. I do not have the familiarity with casual domesticity that some do."

She moved then, because it was that or fling herself at him. And while she was sure that would happen later, there had to be more to all of this, didn't there? Because it felt like there was. It felt like every step they took was surrounded by layers upon layers of meaning.

It felt like they knew each other better than Hannah had ever imagined it was possible to know another person.

But then, on nights like tonight, she would sit and glare at a book and find herself unable to recall if they'd talked substantially about anything.

She walked toward the kitchens, and could hear him

following her. And her head might have been full of fairy tales, but her heart was made of resolve as she went and settled herself at one of the counters and watched as he heated up the food the staff had left for him.

The way he always did.

"Why don't you cook?" she asked.

Hannah saw the way he tensed at that, and regretted the question—

No, she contradicted herself. *You don't regret it. You have nothing to regret. You deserve to know this man who you married, full stop.*

Antonluca took his time preparing the pasta that Hannah had eaten earlier, though he used a pan on the gas range instead of the microwave. She watched as he plated the pasta when it was ready, and if she hadn't known who he was and what he could do, she thought that this would have given it away. There was a certain grace to the way he moved and the way he used utensils. It was obvious even in how he flipped a dish towel over one shoulder, while he moved around the kitchen as if it had been built to suit him in every regard—from the distance to the sink to the easy access to the refrigerator.

But she didn't ask again. She waited, and when he came and took the seat next to her at the counter, she continued to sit there in the quiet that now smelled like garlic and rosemary and was broken only by the sound of his fork against his plate.

For a moment, it was tempting to confuse this for peace.

Maybe it is peace, that same voice inside her argued.

How would you know? Every silence in your parents' house had claws.

He moved the pasta around his plate, then he put his fork down without taking a single bite.

"When I first started cooking," he said, without looking at her, as if he was addressing the pasta before him, "it was all I could think about. Flavors, textures. I liked to play with all of it, as if I was in a conversation that could never end."

Hannah considered that. "I suppose that's what makes it an art."

"I suppose." He looked at her then and she caught her breath because there was something that looked like grief in his eyes. The rest of his face was stern. Unyielding. But the storm in that gray gaze of his made her chest so tight she thought she might start sobbing for whatever it was that had hurt him like this. "And when I could no longer hear the conversation, or take part in it, I tried to fake it. But that was worse."

"What happened?" she asked. As carefully and as quietly as she could.

Because she couldn't help but think that it was unusual that he was answering her at all. She couldn't help but worry that he would come to his senses at any moment, then stop.

"If I knew, I would correct it," was all he said, with a shrug. He returned his attention to the dish before him. "But it is not so terrible. There are other games to play. Other mountains to climb. I'm lucky that I let it sing in me as long as it did. The conversation, or whatever you wish to call it, is no doubt continuing without me."

She sat there, stricken, and watched as he tucked into his meal if he hadn't just told her something deeply heartbreaking.

"Antonluca," she whispered. "Why do you say that so matter-of-factly?"

When it's so sad that you can't do the thing you love, she wanted to say, but didn't dare.

"I started cooking to make money and take care of my family," he told her in that same matter-of-fact way. He glanced at her, there beside him, she could have sworn that he looked confused. "I succeeded at these things. Beyond my wildest imaginings. I have nothing to complain about now. The art was unexpected, and I did nothing to earn it. So I cannot mourn it, now, can I?"

Perhaps he didn't mourn it, but Hannah found that she did as she sat there beside him. It was as if she couldn't help it. It was as if the way he had talked about it had left scars all over her, and she could feel them raised and angry on her skin, puffy and tight and a little bit itchy. And when he finished eating, she watched him clean up after himself with more of that same grace and economy of movement, and that, too, made her heart hurt.

And those scars she knew she really didn't have ached even more.

So when he turned toward her again, she stood. She held out her hands and when he took them, she smiled at him until that storm in his gaze lightened. Until it turned into something else.

She spun around, still holding one of his hands tight, and led him through this castle of his, all the dark rooms and the stern, old stone and then up the stairs of their tower. She tugged him along with her, but stopped at Dominic's room so that she could let her heart break into even more pieces as she watched him go and smooth a hand over their child's head. Then smile at Dominic as he slept, breathing with his whole, small body.

Then she took his hand once more as she led him those last few flights of stairs to their bedroom, and this time, she took charge.

Hannah slid his coat off his broad, muscled shoulders. She pushed him back to sit on the bed, and then she pulled off her own clothes until she was naked there before him. The way his gaze sharpened made her smile.

But when he went to move, she shook her head.

She moved instead, kneeling down before him and running her hands up his muscled thighs until she found his belt. She tilted her head back and looked up at him, holding all of that stormy gray as best she could as she undid his belt, unzipped his trousers, and then reached in to pull out that long, thick length of a cock.

Even touching him made her feel shivery and hot.

Still holding his gaze, Hannah leaned in closer, and licked him, root to tip.

Then she wrapped both of her palms around him and took him deep into her mouth, again and again. Learning him as if he was new to her. Loving him as if he'd let her, if he knew.

And he had never let her do this to completion before, but tonight was going to be different. Hannah would see to it.

His hands moved to her hair, tumbling it down from its clip so that it flowed over her shoulders. He got his hands in it, and knotted it into a kind of strawberry blonde rope that he wrapped around one palm.

She knew it was so that he could look down and see how she took him deep, as if she was trying to swallow him whole.

And when he went to pull her away, she refused to move, only changing the angle of her head so she could look up at him.

"*Diavolessa*—" he growled. "I want—"

"This is what I want," she whispered.

And when she bent close again, she sucked him in deep and felt herself shiver even more as she squeezed her own thighs together. Then was shocked to find herself joining him when he roared out his pleasure and then released himself deep into her throat.

He stayed where he was, panting. And Hannah kissed him, there on his thigh and wherever else she could reach without moving, over and over until he opened up his eyes.

This time with something fierce deep inside them.

"I hope you had fun," he said in a voice so stern it made her smile. And melt. "Because I will."

And it wasn't until much, much later, when she wasn't sure that there was a single part of her that wasn't shredded into glorious bits, that she found herself drifting off toward sleep in his arms.

She was beginning to wonder, while all of this wild, impossible joy charged around through her system, if this wasn't *quite* love, after all. Maybe it was simply that she was addicted to him. To this, as anyone would be.

But if that was true, she didn't think she'd ever get clean. She was pretty sure she would never even try. Maybe, in time, she would stop wondering if she should.

He pulled her closer, pressed a kiss to her temple, and held her to him. Hannah sighed and snuggled in closer.

And had to hope that somehow, she would survive this, as close to intact as possible. Whatever that looked like when he had her heart in his hands, could smash it so easily…and didn't even seem to know it.

CHAPTER TEN

ANTONLUCA MIGHT HAVE forgotten that it was Christmas Eve altogether if it weren't for Dominic, who woke up squealing with glee and could not be contained all throughout his typical morning routine.

"He and Cinzia are going to track Santa Claus all day," Hannah told Antonluca in that very solemn voice she liked to use, her green eyes sparkling with laughter, when she found Dominic particularly entertaining.

Antonluca could never decide if he was charmed by this or something more like saddened, because he knew full well that no one had ever been entertained by *his* antics. Nothing close.

Every day, without even trying to, Hannah taught him something new about how people were meant to operate in the world.

Most of them, he had come to understand, started something like this. With a mother who doted on them and found them fascinating, and went out of her way to find new ways to make their children happy. Or at least safe and reasonably content.

He found it more and more dizzying each time.

Even when the subject at hand was Santa Claus. Or Babbo Natale, as Father Christmas was known in Italy. If he had ever been likely to believe in such a being, he would have gravitated more toward La Befana, the witchlike old woman who was said to dispense gifts or coal on the Epiphany. But Antonluca had not had that sort of childhood.

He had certainly never had cause to believe in benevolent, godlike creatures who dispensed cheer and gifts. Yet looking at his wife's sparkling eyes and his child's excited face, he found himself wishing that he was a different man. That he could be the sort of person who would react to a holiday others loved with pleasure instead of suspicion.

Instead, he had to make himself smile and hope that it looked natural. "I did not realize that Santa Claus could be tracked on his long journey," he said.

Hannah nodded sagely. "But of course we can track Santa Claus. How else would you know if it's time to go to bed and listen for reindeer?"

Then she showed him on her phone the so-called satellite updates of Santa's sleigh, already hard at work in other parts of the world.

It all left Antonluca feeling something like…raw.

It made him wish he hadn't given up his cold walks to the hotel, because he could have used a bit of head-clearing motion just then. But it was the darkest time of the year and the ground was near frozen every day. He didn't like the idea of Hannah driving around, slithering up and down the ancient hills.

"You do know that I grew up in Nebraska, right?" she asked as he mentioned this again on their drive to the hotel that morning. "It's not exactly a tropical island there in the winter. I'm not afraid of bad weather."

"Nor is it an ancient village with slick, stone streets," he replied, though something in him shook a bit, as if the real truth was that he liked her company and it had nothing to do with the state of the roads.

But if that was true, he did not wish to examine it.

He could not.

Because as he kept telling himself that day, he really ought to have been past any of these uncomfortable feelings that kept cropping up. He had married Hannah. He had already started the legal proceedings to name himself Dominic's father on all relevant paperwork. He had also expedited Hannah's dual-citizenship application, though now that she was married to him, he suspected that it would be little more than a formality.

All i's were dotted and t's crossed.

Now all that was left to do was to figure out how he could spend as much time as possible with his son while continuing to maintain his usual schedule. Normally, by the time he spent this much time in any one place, he was more than ready to move on. He liked to come back to Tuscany again and again because it felt like he was a different man here, one with a completely different life. But he never stayed.

Yet every time he sat down to contact his office and have his assistant begin packing out his calendar, he stopped. The idea of more boardrooms and business meetings held no appeal at all.

He told himself it had to be no more than fealty toward Paloma, who had really been such a huge part of his early success. Word of mouth was always helpful, but especially when it was a mouth like Paloma's, with access to some of the most important ears in Europe. Antonluca owed her.

And he had told her that he would stay through Christmas. Surely, he would wake up on the other side of the holiday—which in Italy, of course, did not end until January 6—and be able at last to wash his hands of this episode.

Whatever that looked like, now that he was married and had a son.

He needed to start making decisions...but instead he found himself worrying about Hannah driving on icy roads and whether or not Dominic was appropriately dressed for the cold—things that no one had ever worried about when it was him.

He was surprised he knew how. Because, looking back, he couldn't say that he'd *worried* about his siblings. He'd just...known it was up to him to save them, and so he had.

Christmas Eve was the last night of the Christmas Market, which Antonluca already knew was a vast success. There was no doubt that they would do it again, making it an annual part of the holiday celebrations in the region. People had come from all over and many had enjoyed the drive to and from Florence, the better to experience two versions of Tuscany's finest. The ancient city version versus the ancient village version.

The guests who remained at the hotel, meanwhile, kept pausing in the midst of their holiday to tell staff members how pleased they were. With everything.

"Sir Montgomery Bancroft and his family have said repeatedly that it feels like home," Hannah told him as they conferred outside her office later that day.

Antonluca was distracted, because he was always distracted in her presence. It was another factor in all of this. It was making him feel as if he was outside his own skin. Or possibly it was that he would much prefer to be deep inside her body, at all times.

In any case, they were not in private, so he merely frowned. "Montgomery Bancroft has a vast portfolio of homes in every country on the planet," he said. Perhaps too repressively. "I'm not sure what he means when he says such things."

He expected Hannah to argue with him, but she only looked at him, her eyes too green, for too long.

"Yes, you do," she replied quietly. "You know exactly what it means. We all know what it means."

"Do we, indeed." It came out a bit more dry than he'd intended. "And where is home for you, dare I ask?"

"Here." Hannah shook her head at him. "Where else?" But before he could read too much into that, or ask himself why he *wanted* to read too much into it, she smiled. "Wherever Dominic is, that's home. I guess that includes Cinzia, too. I'm a lucky woman."

But Léontine came up to talk to her then, so Antonluca couldn't ask the next question.

Namely, where he ranked in that tally.

He strode off, telling himself that he was *delighted* that he had been prevented from making such an abject fool of himself. Because that was what this was, clearly. Sheer foolishness.

They were not *dating*. He had married her to give Dominic the family he'd always wanted when he was small. The family he'd wished so fervently that he could have had. That was the beginning and the end of it.

Still, as the day wore on, something about Christmas Eve was winding its way into him, like it or not. There was the mulled wine, bubbling away in the various stations that had been put up around the hotel. It made everything smell of spices and a rich-bodied cheer, and Antonluca had no idea why the scent should affect him so much, given that there had certainly been no *mulled spices* on hand in any of his childhood recollections.

Only his mother's vices and their consequences.

The hotel also offered children's programs, and so it was that some of the richest children on the planet sat about sticking cloves into oranges, like Victorian children from long ago, and then made them into garlands that they hung in the halls.

That, too, filled the hotel with its own complicated, citrusy scent.

The fireplaces were lit. The trees were gleaming. And at eight o'clock that night, while the three restaurants served Christmas Eve delicacies, the staff went into each suite to create a Christmas turndown experience for the guests. There were stockings stuffed with sugar plums, candy canes, Amedei Porcelana chocolates, and Murano glass ornaments, all waiting when the guests returned that evening.

Before they did, there was one more party. This one was an evening cocktail affair, filled with Christmas music, artisan drinks, and dancing. The main ballroom was open, with a vast Christmas dessert buffet, which ranged from *tronchetto di Natale* to *zuccotto* to *panforte*, all traditional Italian sweets, to more international fare, including a chocolate fountain.

The party went until midnight, when the band played "Joy to the World" because it was Christmas Day at last.

Antonluca waited for Hannah in the lobby afterward. It was quiet now, as the guests had all danced their way back to their suites to find real visions of sugar plums awaiting them. All of the trees were lit and sparkling and then Hannah came out from her office, shrugging into her coat, her green eyes brighter than all the evergreens.

He felt something inside of him that he couldn't have explained if his life depended on it. It was too big, too unwieldy. And it seemed to crowd its way through him, taking up all the space, and not caring much if it made him...hurt.

They stepped outside and Hannah tipped her head back, smiling up toward the night sky. Antonluca did the same and found that it was snowing again. Light, airy, insistent flakes of snow spiraling down, dusting the flagstones in front of them.

"I'll admit it," Hannah said, sounding happy and tired. "I really was hoping it would be a white Christmas."

"Come," Antonluca said, not sure why his voice was so dark, so low. Or why that *thing* in him seemed to have no intention of letting go. "Let me take you home."

And that word seemed to glow in the dark as it sat there between them. He couldn't pretend he couldn't feel it. He could see that she did, and he didn't like this bizarre urge he had to...ask her straight-out if she felt at home with him.

He wanted to ask questions he wasn't sure he wanted the answers to, and for no other reason than to simply dig his way deep inside of her and know her better.

It did not occur to him until right then and there, outside in the snow-dusted dark of a very early Christmas morning, that most of his life had been an exercise in keeping people at arm's length. Food was a distant art, when it came time to serve it. The intimacy, for him, was in the kitchen when he'd played with ingredients and garnishes to make everything *exactly right*. The people who then ate his food and felt some kind of kinship with him because of it were nothing to him.

He appreciated them. Of course he did. But that wasn't why he did it. Or why he'd done it, he corrected himself.

But Hannah was different from that. Hannah, and Dominic in turn, were the only two people he had relationships with who he found endlessly fascinating.

His siblings were a duty, still. He would say he was fond of them, in his way, but that had never translated to any kind of closeness. The many people involved in his business ventures were useful, or they didn't last long. That wasn't the same thing as *close*, either.

He wanted to tell Hannah this, as he took her hand and led her to the Range Rover, and then fussed about with getting her coat into the car for perhaps too long as she settled in the passenger seat.

As if she didn't know how to make herself comfortable in a vehicle.

As if he needed to fuss about her like a fool to show her…something. Anything.

Once again, he was acting like a teenage boy who thought he had to sneak his casual touches, but he didn't. Hannah slept in his bed. The last he'd checked, she was even more voracious for his touch now than she had been before.

Because this need between them grew by the day.

Sometimes he thought it might block out the whole

sky, and he wondered why that didn't bother him the way it should.

She was the only life-altering drug he had ever allowed himself.

Tonight there was snow. And it was Christmas. And he would have told anyone who asked how little that meant to him, except...everything seemed different tonight.

He drove them back through the village, making his way over the hills toward the castle, and everything was silent. There were only the bright lights to mark the season as they passed. Everything was hushed. Still.

Expectant, he thought, and now covered in this soft snow.

He had that Christmas carol in his head, but this time, "Silent Night" felt different. Beautiful, yes, but far more complicated than he'd given the song credit for. He was too aware of the dark and of the distance between him and Hannah. He was too taken by the lights everywhere, like emblems of hope.

Though he felt calm and bright, perhaps, within. Though he wasn't sure he had a basis of comparison.

What he did know was this: he wanted nothing more than to reach across the console that separated the two of them. He wanted to put his hands on her—and he understood in that moment that sex was simply a wild, red-hot interpretation of this *thing* inside of him.

And more, that it was in some ways the easier version.

Because whatever it was that swelled in him, so big

and wide he thought he might shatter, he could not name it. He could not fuck it away. He could not make her scream loud enough to drown it out.

Here in this car, in this quiet, sacred night, he could do nothing at all but sit in it.

And it only seemed to grow bigger and heavier as he drove them up to the castle and parked where he always did, on the cracked old stones in the ancient courtyard.

When they got out of the car, the night was, if anything, more hushed than before. It seemed at such odds with all that noise inside of him, and the insistent, silent snow.

He waited for Hannah to smile, or tip her head back again, or say something...

But she didn't. She looked up at the castle and then she ducked her head again, and he had the strangest feeling that she was deliberately concealing her expression from him—though he couldn't think why she would do such a thing. Surely they had passed the point where she had to conceal her actual feelings behind a polite mask. Certainly, even if she had to do such things at work to remain professional, she didn't have to do it here.

Did she?

He followed after her as she walked into the castle, and once inside, there was no mistaking it. He could see her face in the lights of the entry hall.

She looked sad. His heart began to kick at him, hard.

Her eyes were overbright, and if he wasn't mistaken,

that was moisture he could see gathering there along the rims.

Antonluca decided, then and there, that what pounded in him, what swelled and grew too unwieldy and took him over like a wave, was *temper*.

Because it had to be temper. Because whatever was happening here, he couldn't bear it.

"What is the matter?" he asked, and it was only when she jumped a bit at that, looking startled, that it occurred to him that his approach could have been a bit softer.

"Nothing is the matter," she said. But she lied.

Because even as she said it, a tear formed and tracked its way down her cheek.

And that unwieldy weight inside of him shifted, hard. He nearly staggered under it. Instead, he reached over and scowled at her as he brushed that tear away from her cheek. He stared down at it, then at her, as if she had betrayed him.

Again, something in him reminded him. *She has betrayed you* again, *and what will keep her from continuing?*

"Why the hell aren't you happy?" he demanded.

He had never heard himself sound so rough.

Hannah's mouth dropped open and he saw a mix of reactions move across her face—but there was something sharper still in her gaze. He reached out again because another tear threatened, but she caught his wrist as he went to wipe it away.

"Why aren't you?" she asked.

Her voice was barely above a whisper, yet Antonluca heard it everywhere, as if from on high. He could feel it drum its way deep into his bones, as if the noise inside of him had summoned precisely *this*.

A question like that.

A question that no one should dare ask, not of him. He wasn't the one weeping in a castle. He wasn't the one whose marriage had changed the entire course of his life, from a tiny rented cottage to a life of ease, and was still unaccountably *sad* on a holiday even he knew was supposed to be *joyful*.

"I am perfectly happy," he told her, not managing to keep the note of arrogant astonishment—or perhaps it was straight outrage, now that he thought about it, because how dare she—out of his voice. "I couldn't spend all my money if I dedicated the rest of my life to the attempt. I bought myself a castle on a whim. I will never have to want for anything, ever again, for as long as I live."

"That's your portfolio. I wasn't talking about that."

It was as if he couldn't hear her. Or he couldn't stop, anyway. "I raised not only myself, but each and every one of my siblings out of poverty," he threw at her, his words like bullets. "I created an entire corporate entity to make certain that they were taken care of for the rest of their days. I didn't simply pull them from the street, I made them rich, too."

Hannah shook her head, still gripping his wrist, her

tearstained face far too close to his. "You're still talking about money."

"I understand that your family has not treated you the way you would like," he thundered at her, full now with a righteous indignation that he had been holding inside him for as long as he could remember. Since he'd been a kid washing dishes. "I'm not discounting that, but it isn't the same thing. It is a privilege to have the space and time, not to mention the full belly, to worry about your *feelings*."

He had wanted to say that, to a great many people, for a very long time.

"But you are safe now," Hannah replied quietly, her green eyes direct and sure. "You have all the privileges in the world, don't you? Castles. Private jets. A whole empire. Ample time to dig into your own feelings without worrying about starving, I'd think. So what about them? How do you *feel*, Antonluca?"

"I don't know what you mean. I am Antonluca Aniello. Why should I feel anything but perfectly fine?"

She dropped his wrist then, and that was how he realized that he'd forgotten she was holding it. Then she crossed her arms, and did not shift her gaze from his. Not even for a second.

"There are many ways that I might describe you, Antonluca," she said in that same too-quiet, too-sure way. "But *fine* isn't one of them."

"I have nothing to complain about," he threw at her, and he didn't like the fact that his heart seemed to be working overtime in his chest. He didn't like that he was entertaining this discussion in the first place when she was the one who was crying, for no reason. He was certain that it was her fault that he had this great mess of unwieldy nonsense inside of him in the first place. "If I do find that I have something to complain about, I fix it. Immediately. Or I have someone else do it for me. I have no issues, with anything, at all."

But Hannah was not the least bit cowed by this unassailable bit of knowledge. On the contrary, she leaned in closer—and the high heels she was wearing allowed her to put her face almost directly into his.

"You live in an empty castle," she told him, enunciating each word so that it felt like a slap. "It's like you're already a ghost."

When he only stared back at her, somehow as shocked by that as if she had hauled off and slapped him, she kept going. He could see the glitter of temper in her gaze—or maybe it wasn't temper at all. Maybe it was some other passion that he couldn't understand, that the gigantic weight inside him was still sitting on.

"You have nothing personal in this entire pile of old stone," she said. "Not one thing."

He scoffed at that. "Says the woman without a single personal item in the office where she spends most of her days."

"That is an *office*," Hannah replied, shaking her head a little. "It's also a job that I started while pregnant. It was necessary for me to make it clear that my being a mother in no way inhibits the work that I do. You've been in my cottage. You saw exactly how it was decorated."

He made a noncommittal sort of noise, and even told himself that he could not possibly remember the decor of a cottage he had rushed to get her out of—

But she laughed at whatever expression she saw on his face. "I know you saw all those pictures on the wall. Baby pictures of Dominic. Dominic and me. Dominic and Cinzia. Happy moments from a happy life, Antonluca. But you don't have any of that, do you? Not a single indication that you have ever been alive at all, anywhere, with anyone."

"I apologize," he said, moving in closer to her, "if I have somehow made you feel less than *alive*, Hannah."

And he reached out for her, a half-formed thought chasing through him. That he would crush his mouth to hers, set them both on fire, and see how they burned. Maybe that would prove...whatever needed proving here.

But instead, when he pulled her close, she melted against him.

As if there was no anger here. As if he was the only one fighting, shadowboxing his own apparition.

It seemed to take his knees out from under him, so when he fit his mouth to hers, it was something else.

It was a kiss, but it *ached*.

It was sweet and sacred. It was *impossible*—

And, suddenly, he understood far more than he

wanted to about that weight inside him, and his own foolish heart, and the sheer magic of this.

Of her.

He kissed her again and again, never getting any deeper, never pushing, because this already felt like too much.

This felt like home, in all the ways he least wanted it to.

It felt... He felt...

He couldn't let himself get there.

But she was the one who pulled away, and stood there a moment, her fingertips pressed to his hard jaw. Her breath still heavy and tangled with his.

"Don't you see?" she whispered. "You live like you're in prison, Antonluca. Like you're serving time for some hideous crime and I don't think you know what that crime is any more than I do. But I do know this. Dominic and I are now serving time with you. Right here in this prison you're so proud of, with its bare walls and its cold, harsh stone."

"Hannah—" he began, trying to find some way to explain all of that mess inside of him. All of that unbearable weight. "Hannah, I—"

"And I can't bear it," she told him, her voice solemn and this time, her gaze, too. "Because I love you."

"You can't," he growled at her even as everything inside of him seemed to take a seismic hit. "That's not possible."

But as he watched, Hannah shifted back. She wiped

at her eyes, and she even offered something like a smile when all he could see was the resolve behind it. Her spine straightened and he remembered when he'd first seen her in his restaurant in New York. She'd held her shoulders just like this.

As if warding off a terrible blow.

"I'm afraid that it's more than possible," she said, in that calm way of hers that made everything inside him seem to freeze. Then turn into a sharp pain that made him want to double over. Yet she showed no signs of stopping. "I love you, Antonluca. I suspect I always have. And I don't have the slightest idea what will become of any of us, because no matter how pretty you make the prison, it will always be this at heart." She looked around, managing to take in the whole of the castle, and then she slammed that green gaze at him. "It doesn't matter how big it is. It's still a cell. It will always be a cell, Antonluca, until you figure out a way to open it up, and set yourself free."

"I don't have any such need or desire," he began, because that was always his knee-jerk reaction to...anything.

"And if you can't do it for yourself," she said quietly, cutting him off that easily. And in such a dignified way that he thought she might as well pull one of those stones from the wall behind her and smash it straight through his chest, where his heart ought to be. "Do it for your child's sake. Do you really want him to grow up and be like you?"

Maybe, he thought in a daze, she really had crushed him with a rock.

But apparently not, because while he stood there—not sure how it was he wasn't staggering back and crashing to the hard floor beneath them—she simply turned away. Then dashed up the stairs, leaving him to pick up the pieces on his own.

Assuming there was anything left of him but ash.

Yet all he could do was stand there, staring around him as if he'd gone blind. As if he had suddenly found himself in a place he didn't know, unable to figure out how he'd gotten himself there.

Part of him wanted simply to chase her upstairs because he knew there was nothing they couldn't work out in bed together.

But he couldn't seem to move.

It was as if his feet had turned to stone, too.

And despite himself, despite everything, he felt the truth bear down upon him like another impossible weight.

He had to let go and he didn't know how.

That was the prison she was talking about. He'd been born in it and he'd never left it. He had never, ever let go of the place he'd come from. He had never forgotten, no matter how high he'd flown, how hard he'd fought to get away from those dirty streets, far more cruel than anyone liked to imagine.

But she wasn't wrong. He hadn't been near those streets—or any streets—in longer than he'd ever been on them. He had done everything he'd vowed to himself that he would do when he was young and angry and scared—and then some.

He had saved every damned person he could on his way out, except himself.

He took a step and found himself sagging so badly that he had to hold himself up against the nearest wall. It was as if every single illusion he'd ever held on to had crumbled, just like that.

And once again, the truth was so bright and so obvious that it was painful.

It was also simple.

He'd been fighting against it all this time because fighting was what he knew how to do. But there was one way to give his son the life he truly deserved. And while he was at it, treat his wife the way she deserved, too.

And maybe, just maybe, he would find a way to treat himself the same way.

No bare stone walls. No haunted castles.

Imagine, he asked himself, the way he hadn't in so very long now, *how much flavor your life could have if you allowed it?*

If he wanted her heart, he had to locate his own.

If he wanted to live, to truly *live* and to *be alive* in every way that mattered, he could not keep himself apart the way he'd been doing for years now. Life, like a perfect dish, was texture and flavor in an endless conversation with one another, and he didn't know why it was he'd locked himself away for this long.

But he did know this. Hannah had given him an opportunity to resurrect himself.

And it seemed to him a stark and unmistakable truth that if he did not do it now, he never would.

If he did not do it now, he would be little more than the stone walls that surrounded him. He was already more than halfway there. For all intents and purposes, he was a ghost right now.

He straightened on the wall. He looked around his castle, and his life, and his own messy heart, with new eyes.

Eyes Hannah had opened, painful as that was.

Eyes he could not close again. Not now that he could finally see.

And not that he had the slightest idea how to fix what he hadn't even realized he'd broken.

But he stood a little straighter and he reminded himself that he was Antonluca Aniello, who had made an empire out of thin air when he'd been little more than a child. He'd made it look *easy*.

So there was no telling what he could do now.

CHAPTER ELEVEN

AFTER SHE'D CREPT in to relieve the staff member who'd babysat Dominic and assured herself that her son, at least, was sleeping soundly, Hannah cried herself to sleep and then slept badly.

And with all the things she'd said to Antonluca in the middle of her typical Christmas Eve heartache—though, usually, it was less pointed and more of a general *what will become of me* ringing in her head—she decided once she woke up the next morning that she was afraid to actually admit she was awake.

Because she wasn't sure she wanted to get up and face the mess she'd helped make last night.

Instead, she lay there with the covers pulled up over her head. She was keenly aware that Antonluca had not joined her in bed last night, at any point, for the first time in their admittedly short marriage.

Hannah didn't like to think about what that could mean.

And so when she heard Dominic begin to sing in his room, it felt like a relief. Even if it was still dreadfully early.

At least this part was perfectly normal.

She poked her head out from under the covers and, sure enough, she could hear his little feet moving across the floor, and up the few stairs the way he liked to do now. When he made it to the side of her bed, she leaned over and scooped him up, kissing him all over his face as he laughed and squealed and babbled in a mix of Italian and English to say the same thing.

It was Christmas, did she know? Because he was certain, as only small children could be, that Santa had come.

"Do you think you were a good boy?" Hannah asked him, very seriously.

His gray eyes widened in outrage, and he was so much like his father that it hurt.

"*Mamma, lo ero. Lo so!*" he cried at once. Then he said it again, in English, in case she needed a translation. "I was good, Mama. I know I was!"

She kissed him all over his face. "I know you were, *angioletto*," she agreed. "You always are."

Hannah had planned out their Christmas morning in advance, fairly certain that her husband was not likely to wake up filled with anything resembling Christmas cheer. The good news, to her mind, was that Dominic was too little to expect anything. He didn't have any picture in his head about what Christmas *ought* to be. So she had decided she would make it as relaxed as possible. Breakfast. Gifts. Later, she would take him over to

Cinzia's, and perhaps they would join in the Christmas meal that Cinzia and her family always had.

This was almost exactly what she had done last year, and she'd loved it.

But as she got up from the bed, her attention was caught by the sunrise outside the windows and the beautiful, brightly colored light that spread across the sky and highlighted something else.

The fact that it was still snowing.

"Look," she told Dominic. "It's a white Christmas. Just like the song."

She pulled on her own clothes and then brought Dominic down to his room so that he could get dressed, too, since he liked to kick off his pajamas in the night. They sang "White Christmas" the whole time—or she did, anyway, and he hummed along, with more enthusiasm than tune.

It was only when Dominic insisted on walking down the stairs of the tower, which meant that she had to keep herself angled in front of him in case he took a tumble, that Hannah realized there was something else magical about the morning.

It wasn't simply the snow outside and a happy little boy. There was a glorious, sweet scent, everywhere.

She thought she had to be hallucinating cinnamon rolls.

But when they got to the bottom of the stairs and made it out of the tower and into the rest of the castle, both she and Dominic stared around in wonder.

Because *this* castle wasn't the one she'd been in last night, before bed.

Overnight, as if by the wave of a magic wand, it was like they were in a completely different castle altogether.

"What happened?" asked her sweet little boy. "Was it Santa?"

"Maybe," Hannah said.

She had an idea who it might be, other than Santa Claus—but it seemed so outlandish. So deeply impossible. So much so that she scooped Dominic up and settled him on her hip because she needed to hold on to *something*.

Then, together, they wandered through the main floor of the castle as if it was new.

Because in every way that mattered, it was.

In the few hours left of the night after she'd run upstairs, the coldest and most lonely castle in Italy had become…cozy.

There were rugs everywhere, tapestries on the walls, and evergreen trees festooned with lights. The rooms they passed were no longer empty. Instead, they were brimming with comfortable-looking furniture, fires in every fireplace, music playing—Christmas carols, no less—and all of the photographs that had been in her cottage, the photographs that hadn't made it to the castle when Antonluca had moved her the night of their wedding, were displayed.

They were everywhere. Like this was their home.

Like all of this was *theirs*, too.

Not just a cell to occupy while they all did time together.

She found her way into Antonluca's only previously furnished room and found that even it had suffered a makeover. Now it sported a big Christmas tree in one corner, lavishly decorated, with piles of perfectly wrapped presents laid beneath it.

Once again, Hannah felt her eyes get heavy with emotion because this looked more like the Christmas of her dreams than any she'd ever had. Back home in Nebraska, even though everyone had always been on their best behavior on a day like this, there would always be *undercurrents*. Muttering about agendas and *high-falutin' airs* and dire warnings not to touch the cookies lest the cookie exchange be *ruined*.

Things she'd ignored because she'd wanted to enjoy Christmas.

Yet somehow Antonluca had dug into her finest, most dearly held daydreams, and had provided her with every single one of them come true.

And still, there was that marvelous smell of dough and sugar and cinnamon, making her stomach grumble.

She left Dominic to leap around in glee at all of the Christmas splendor and followed her nose back into the kitchen.

Where she stopped dead once again.

Because Antonluca was there.

But more amazing, he was cooking.

The counter was filled with platters of food, and even at a quick glance she could see that he had covered what looked like every possible Christmas tradition around. There were piles of fragrant cinnamon rolls, there were bacon dishes and eggs, hot chocolate, sweets, panettone and *pandoro*, and many dishes she couldn't identify at a glance.

She could hardly believe her eyes.

And when he turned around from the cooking range to face her, she caught her breath.

Because this was an Antonluca she recognized, but not usually outside of their bed. This was a man made of passion, and a wild, beautiful heart. She could see it in him. She could certainly see it in the food he'd prepared.

As if he'd found that magic in him again.

And she understood, as if he'd reached in and touched her heart with his, that he was showing her his love in the only way he could.

She understood other things then. Like why he had stepped back from cooking. Because it must have felt unrequited to him, all this intense and glorious *love* he had in him, especially after it had performed the task he'd claimed he'd learned it for.

Because he had never allowed himself space to do anything simply because he *loved* it.

That wasn't in his vocabulary. That was anathema to the street kid who had simply needed to survive. She understood that now.

But here he was, cooking for her. And their son. On Christmas morning in that cold prison he had turned into a home overnight.

He stared at her from across the room, and Hannah had never seen this man look so…out of his depth.

He stood tall, his gray eyes a kind of storm she'd never seen before. For a long moment, he only stared at her and then he looked, almost helplessly, at the counter piled high with food.

With his art. His joy. *His love*.

"I didn't know what you would like," he said, his voice gruff and stiff and not like his at all. "So I made everything."

"Antonluca," Hannah managed to get out, though her throat was tight, holding his gaze the way she wished she really could reach over and hold him, too, "I love you, too."

Dominic came rushing in then, squealing with delight, and ran straight to his father. Giving Hannah the piercing joy of watching her child and her husband bask in each other, as if love had always been a feast. As if it was supposed to be, not the crumbs she'd hoarded away in her family's house.

She found that she had never been so hungry in all her life. Hannah went to the counter and fixed herself a plate. Then found tears rolling down her cheeks as she tasted, one bite and then the next, pure *love*.

Salty. Sweet. Perfectly fluffy, gloriously dense. It was everything. It was the dance of flavor on her tongue, it was spice when needed, and the lightest, airiest pastry imaginable. It was meringues with perfect peaks and fluffy eggs baked into fragrant quiches. Perfect hot chocolate and decadently strong coffee.

Antonluca shooed them out of the kitchen and brought trays into the room that Hannah supposed was now their living room, where Antonluca and Hannah got to be parents watching an overexcited toddler amuse himself beneath the Christmas tree for the first time while they feasted and laughed.

And when Dominic had to take what would likely be his first sugar crash nap of the day, they found each other there on the floor. Surrounded by wrapping paper, a crackling fire, and watchful Christmas tree, they knelt together, gripped each other's hands, and basked in each other, too.

"Hannah," he said, holding her hands between his. "My beautiful, impossible Hannah, I wanted to show you the only way I could. I don't know what love is, but I know how it tastes."

"So do I," she said, and kissed him.

He kissed her back, but then he sent her apart from him again. He smoothed his hands over her cheeks, letting his fingers find their way into her hair.

"I know how love tastes," he said again. "A hint of sugar and the complication of the perfect spice. You, Hannah. And you have brought me more love than I could possibly deserve. You have given me you and our beautiful son. Somehow, last night, you even brought me back to my food, too."

"It's okay to love things," she whispered. "It's all

right to let the act of loving them transform you. It's not a weakness."

"I didn't know love," he told her urgently, pressing kisses to her brow, her cheeks, her nose. "But I discovered *food* and I poured myself into it, and I saved almost everyone I know. And for those I could not save, like my mother, it was like a tonic while they were there. And so for me, love became the fighting. And once it was not necessary for me to fight, I could not love, either."

"And yet," Hannah said quietly, like a vow, "look at how you love me. And our son."

"Entirely because of you," he said, and his voice was rough again, but his eyes gleamed like silver. "Because you told the truth to that tabloid just as, last night, you told me the truth straight to my face. I don't need to be a circus act. I don't need to keep myself in prison for crimes I did not commit. I cannot blame my mother for what few choices she had before her, but it's not my fault I couldn't save her from it. Sometimes, if I'm really honest, I think she didn't want to be saved."

"Sometimes," Hannah agreed, "we all have to save ourselves."

"You say that," Antonluca said quietly, tucking a bit of her hair behind her ear, "but I am quite certain, Hannah Hansen of Nebraska, that you are the only one in all the world who could have saved me. And you did, without my even knowing it."

"I promise you this," she said, smiling at him. "I always will."

"And what I promise you in return, *diavolessa*," he

said, "my little devil of a bride, is that I will never turn my back on this life. I will always choose you and our family first. And I will learn how to love you all in a way that does not come with strings, but feels the way this morning tastes. Right. Endless. Ours."

"Merry Christmas, my beautiful husband," Hannah whispered, no longer caring that the tears were pouring freely down her face, not when she was smiling so wide and so hard that her cheeks hurt. "I have to tell you, this is the best one yet."

He pulled her into his arms and settled her on his lap, so he could kiss her a little more thoroughly. But not too wildly, not yet. Not now. Not while Dominic slept there beside them, and he supposed that he would learn to love this, too.

The sweet anticipation, because he knew that they would end every night together. That even if they were separated for a day or two here and there, they would always have this.

Home.

Wherever they were together, that's where he would be.

And they would play with these flames for the rest of their days.

"Just you wait," he promised her, kissing her like it was the first time, because with Hannah, it always was. "I haven't even started."

CHAPTER TWELVE

ANTONLUCA HAD SPENT his life defying all odds, building empires and making the world his, and still, allowing himself to be open and vulnerable and completely in love with Hannah and the family they made was by far the hardest.

It was also the easiest.

He summoned all of his siblings to the castle for the Epiphany, six days into the New Year.

They all came grumbling and complaining, no doubt thinking that this would be some sort of business lecture.

But instead, Antonluca threw them a proper Christmas. He did all the cooking. He refused to discuss business. And most of all, he showed them that they, too, could risk opening their hearts.

"Assuming," he told Rocco, his mouth curving, "that you have one, little brother. As that is not entirely clear."

His brother responded with a very crude rejoinder that made everyone laugh, Antonluca especially.

And of all the things that he'd given his siblings in

the course of their lives, he thought that Christmas was the best. It wasn't money. It wasn't security. It was love.

Finally, after all these years, it was just as simple as that. *Love*.

And as if he'd shown them the way, each and every one of them shifted after that.

It wasn't like night and day, but within five years—all of them with their new Christmas tradition in the castle in Tuscany—all of them had families of their own.

Even Rocco.

Hannah took Antonluca home with her to Nebraska, later that first year. She showed him all around and introduced him and Dominic to her family, who immediately embarrassed her by being precisely as oddly antagonistic as she'd told him they were.

He was unimpressed—and he thought his reaction to them was validating for her. It wasn't just her. They just…weren't kind or particularly nice to Hannah. There was no reason or rationale. It was just them.

All except her sister, that was, who was delighted to meet her nephew and brother-in-law and who, Antonluca had thought then, might actually be worth maintaining a connection with.

And Hannah, with that big heart of hers, couldn't resist. But this time, Antonluca intended to be there to defend his wife if necessary. It was the very least he could do—and he was happy that her sister didn't make that necessary. Their parents' oddness didn't bleed into the new relationship the sisters had developed.

"This," Hannah told him after the first time her sister and her family came to Italy, "is better than I ever dreamed it could be."

He held her close, out there in the summer sun with the glory of Tuscany all around and the children playing like the lifelong friends these cousins would become.

"*Diavolessa*, I keep telling you. We are only getting started." He kissed her temple and breathed her in. "Just wait."

And in the meantime, they let their own hearts expand.

Their first daughter was born at the end of their first summer, as if they'd been trying to make her that Christmas. Maybe they had been. Antonluca knew he certainly hadn't been doing anything to prevent it.

They named her Paloma, and did their very best to make sure that she lived up to her namesake. Then they had two more boys, each one perfectly themselves.

They also built hotel experiences that felt like homes, filled with restaurants that served food like love, and the best part of that was they did it together. There was no separation between family and work.

It was simply *them*. It was the Circo Aniello, the Aniello circus. It was their brand, but more, it was who they were.

Art and joy, love and life, work and so much play, and it was all theirs.

And every night for the rest of their lives—or as close to every night as was possible—Antonluca picked up his wife and carried her over the threshold of their bedroom so he could lay her down on their bed.

Then take his time reminding them both of their wedding night, by making it better.

Over and over and over again, better and better still, until forever melted like sugar all over them.

Then they began again, because they were still getting started.

And the best was yet to come.

* * * * *

*Did you fall in love with
An Heir for Christmas?
Then you're sure to enjoy these
other sensational stories
by Caitlin Crews!*

Greek's Enemy Bride
Carrying a Sicilian Secret
Kidnapped for His Revenge
Her Accidental Spanish Heir
Forbidden Greek Mistress

Available now!

Get up to 4 Free Books!

**We'll send you 2 free books from each series you try
PLUS a free Mystery Gift.**

FREE Value Over **$25**

Both the **Harlequin Presents** and **Harlequin Medical Romance** series feature exciting stories of passion and drama.

YES! Please send me 2 FREE novels from Harlequin Presents or Harlequin Medical Romance and my FREE gift (gift is worth about $10 retail). After receiving them, if I don't wish to receive any more books, I can return the shipping statement marked "cancel." If I don't cancel, I will receive 6 brand-new larger-print novels every month and be billed just $7.19 each in the U.S., or $7.99 each in Canada, or 4 brand-new Harlequin Medical Romance Larger-Print books every month and be billed just $7.19 each in the U.S. or $7.99 each in Canada, a savings of 20% off the cover price. It's quite a bargain! Shipping and handling is just 50¢ per book in the U.S. and $1.25 per book in Canada.* I understand that accepting the 2 free books and gift places me under no obligation to buy anything. I can always return a shipment and cancel at any time. The free books and gift are mine to keep no matter what I decide.

Choose one:
- ☐ **Harlequin Presents Larger-Print** (176/376 BPA G36Y)
- ☐ **Harlequin Medical Romance** (171/371 BPA G36Y)
- ☐ **Or Try Both!** (176/376 & 171/371 BPA G36Z)

Name (please print)

Address   Apt. #

City   State/Province   Zip/Postal Code

Email: Please check this box ☐ if you would like to receive newsletters and promotional emails from Harlequin Enterprises ULC and its affiliates. You can unsubscribe anytime.

Mail to the Harlequin Reader Service:
IN U.S.A.: P.O. Box 1341, Buffalo, NY 14240-8531
IN CANADA: P.O. Box 603, Fort Erie, Ontario L2A 5X3

Want to explore our other series or interested in ebooks? Visit www.ReaderService.com or call 1-800-873-8635.

---

*Terms and prices subject to change without notice. Prices do not include sales taxes, which will be charged (if applicable) based on your state or country of residence. Canadian residents will be charged applicable taxes. Offer not valid in Quebec. This offer is limited to one order per household. Books received may not be as shown. Not valid for current subscribers to the Harlequin Presents or Harlequin Medical Romance series. All orders subject to approval. Credit or debit balances in a customer's account(s) may be offset by any other outstanding balance owed by or to the customer. Please allow 4 to 6 weeks for delivery. Offer available while quantities last.

Your Privacy—Your information is being collected by Harlequin Enterprises ULC, operating as Harlequin Reader Service. For a complete summary of the information we collect, how we use this information and to whom it is disclosed, please visit our privacy notice located at https://corporate.harlequin.com/privacy-notice. Notice to California Residents – Under California law, you have specific rights to control and access your data. For more information on these rights and how to exercise them, visit https://corporate.harlequin.com/california-privacy. For additional information for residents of other U.S. states that provide their residents with certain rights with respect to personal data, visit https://corporate.harlequin.com/other-state-residents-privacy-rights/.

HPHM25